# THE QUEEN
## NEW SHORT FICT

Edited and Introduced by Marshall Moore and Xu Xi

Critical, Cultural and Communications Press
London
2014

*The Queen of Statue Square: New Short Fiction from Hong Kong,*
edited by Marshall Moore and Xu Xi.

First published in Great Britain by Critical, Cultural and
Communications Press, Nottingham, 2014.

Reprinted 2017.

Cover photograph by Jérémy, reproduced by permission
(**https://www.flickr.com/photos/than777/**).

Cover design by Hannibal.

ISBN 9781905510436

# CONTENTS

# INTRODUCTION
# Marshall Moore and Xu Xi

## Who is a Hong Kong people?

What is Hong Kong identity, and what do the stories in this anthology have to do with it? These questions surfaced when we were preparing the call for submissions for this book. Originally intending it to be part of the World Englishes series published by CCC Press, we set out to keep a World Englishes (as it is understood in the field of linguistics) focus. After much discussion with the publisher and series editor, we settled on the following definition for the call for submissions:

> Contributors should ordinarily be residents of Hong Kong and stories should have Hong Kong or its culture as a theme or setting. The series is designed to represent Anglophone writing in a linguistic context in which English is not the sole or dominant language and to convey a strong sense of place and particular culture. By implication, the volume is not intended as a vehicle for expatriate writers who happen simply to live there temporarily; neither is this a collection of Hong Kong Chinese diaspora writing. However, Hong Kong's unusual political situation—it has never been an independent nation or city-state—gives rise to an Anglophone writing that departs from the usual colonial/postcolonial literature. Therefore both expatriate and diaspora authors might, in some instances, render a more persuasive contemporary fiction than a 'native' resident.

If Hong Kong were easy to simplify, this would have simplified things. Who is a 'native' resident? Or, to put the question another way, who is a 'Hong Kong people', a common second-language error here that raises interesting and rather profound questions when one unpacks the meaning underneath the Chinglish. Can people other than Cantonese-speaking Chinese fit the definition? Questions like these, as they have played out in the courts and the media, have led to shouting in the streets. And without the editors explicitly naming identity as a focus of this book (it is, after all, a fiction anthology, not a collection of essays in one of the social sciences), identity manifested as a theme in every story we accepted and quite a few that we did not.

At the time of this writing, there were protests over the HKSAR government's rejection of an application to establish a new TV network. This may sound tangential at first, but in fact it has everything to do with the porous, parlous state of Hong Kong identity. Ricky Wong Wai-kay, a businessman who had already established local broadband and telecom companies, spent several years—and quite a bit of his personal fortune—laying the groundwork to establish Hong Kong Television Network Limited (HKTV). When the government turned him down, for reasons not publicly announced, uproar ensued: thousands of people marched wearing black T-shirts, not just to show solidarity with Wong but to demand accountability for the decision.[1] Among the general population, HKTV's launch has been seen as welcome news. Wong's intention has been and remains to provide an alternative to the rather anodyne offerings served up by Hong Kong's legacy networks, which tend to feature romantic dramas with recycled plots, manic variety shows, and carefully worded news broadcasts that avoid touchy matters like Tibet, the political status of Taiwan, and the events that took place in Tiananmen Square.

What was going on, then? What prompted the government's refusal to issue Wong a licence to establish HKTV (which he had already done, presumably not having expected the government's decision)? There was much speculation that—as is rumored about many unpopular government decisions in Hong Kong—Beijing had acted behind the scenes to block Wong's application.

[1] http://www.thestandard.com.hk/breaking_news_detail.asp?id=41936&icid=a&d_str=.

Taking into account Hong Kong's political status and Beijing's well-known impatience with matters pertaining to Chinese sovereignty, this theory is perhaps not as outrageous as it might at first appear. Hong Kong's entertainment industry (film in particular) has long been a locus of local identity, and to a significant degree it has now been subsumed by the wealthy mainland. Case in point: a number of Hong Kong's most prominent filmmakers have headed north, lured by generous funding and offers of studio space from municipalities like Beijing and Hangzhou eager to invest in cultural capital.[2] According to the terms of the 1997 handover, Hong Kong is to be fully absorbed into the mainland Chinese polity in a few more decades. According to the logic of the conspiracy theorists, Beijing is already chipping away at Hong Kong's identity. Thus, when 2047 rolls around, there will be no discernible differences left, at least in theory. When one further considers Beijing's propensity for long-term planning, these accusations of deliberate cultural erosion seem less shocking, even rather pragmatic. To what extent is this just the rantings of the conspiracy nutters? To what extent is it the transparent hand of the Chinese Communist Party? This is a question for history. There are no answers at this time, merely a conversation—or an ongoing argument, as it were, that erupts at regular intervals on Hennessy Road with barricades and loudspeakers.

Hong Kong is unique, one result of which is that the criteria for who should rightfully be considered a Hong Kong people are difficult to pin down. What is Hong Kong exactly? The question is more complicated than it sounds. To much of the world, it seems to be a city in southern China, but this is an oversimplification that omits much that is important about the territory's unusual political status. Hong Kong, like its smaller neighbour Macau, is a Special Administrative Region (SAR) of China, a former colony (British, in Hong Kong's case; Portuguese in Macau's) that was handed back to Beijing in 1997 (Macau in 1999). However, there is still more to it than that. Hong Kong is

---

[2] http://variety.com/2013/biz/news/hong-kong-filmmakers-reflect-on-the-territorys-multiple-identities-1200806244/.

not directly governed by Beijing: instead, it operates much like an independent city-state, with Singapore serving as a point of comparison. (It should be noted that Singapore has been an independent state since 1965.) Hong Kong issues its own passports and currency, writes and enacts its own laws, independently joins international organisations like the World Bank and the International Olympic Committee, and so on. Thus, Hong Kong may belong to China, but it is no more 'China' than, say, Gibraltar or Bermuda are 'Britain'.

So who is a Hong Kong person, then? An important distinction is often lost: even though there is significant overlap between Hong Kong identity and Chinese ethnicity, they are different for reasons of history, culture, and law. The SAR's longstanding status as port, business hub, safe haven, and entrepôt means that Hong Kong is a transient space. What's more, the territory's Basic Law—the document that functions as Hong Kong's Constitution—provides for permanent residency after seven years, an arrangement unusual in Asia.[3] According to the 2011 census, 94% of the population is Han Chinese. Indonesians and Filipinos are almost tied for second place with about 135,000 each, Caucasians about 55,000, and there are significant populations of Indians, Pakistanis, Nepalese, Japanese, and Thais.[4] Many of these families, particularly the Indians and Filipinos, have been resident in Hong Kong for generations. In the run-up to the 1997 Handover, hundreds of thousands of Hong Kong people emigrated. The Tiananmen Square massacre was still fresh in the public mind, and many feared what the mainland government might be capable of. What's more, many other countries opened their doors to these would-be emigrants with special residency schemes and programmes.[5] Even so, once it was established that tanks would not roll in the streets after the Handover, many of these emigrants opted to maintain homes in

---

[3] http://www.gov.hk/en/residents/immigration/idcard/roa/geninfor. htm.

[4] http://www.had.gov.hk/rru/english/info/info_dem.html.

[5] http://www.repository.law.indiana.edu/cgi/viewcontent.cgi?article= 1069&context=ijgls.

Hong Kong and return regularly for weeks or months at a time. In other words, it is a mistake to conflate Cantonese-speaking Han Chinese ethnicity and Hong Kong identity. And Hong Kong's unique diaspora is too variegated and too connected to be ruled out without closer examination.

## Stories in the present volume

Even when one is quite familiar with the potential if-then scenarios, the identity question is still difficult to settle, as we may see in the stories. There are always loopholes, exceptions, obstacles, and areas of ontological weirdness. In Nury Vittachi's 'The Queen of Statue Square', Hong Kong's domestic helpers—most of whom are Filipinas legally barred from obtaining the aforementioned permanent residency no matter how much time they have spent in the SAR[6]—have educated themselves and, on the occasion of the 2047 'second handover' to mainland China, become a force to be reckoned with. In many ways, this story is a perfect encapsulation of everything this book is trying to say. Vittachi himself is one of Hong Kong's most prominent authors, one without whom no collection of Hong Kong short fiction would be complete. Yet he is a long-time expat, originally from Sri Lanka. He and his English wife have adopted and raised three Chinese children. If he isn't a Hong Kong person, no one is.

In 'Make-Believe', Yeung Chak Yan examines the concept of identity as it relates to a young Hongkonger. We meet a young boy who may or may not be the reincarnation of a woman's deceased brother. The protagonist, a young woman who has gone to the UK for university study, has returned to Hong Kong for a holiday visit. At home, she discovers her mother taking care of the aforementioned boy—who seems to remember things that the dead child experienced. Who (or what) is this boy, and what (or who) does he want? What underpins the story, and what appears elsewhere in the book, is a reflection on how common it

[6] http://www.reuters.com/article/2012/03/28/us-hongkong-abode-filipino-idUSBRE82R0CB20120328.

is for young Hongkongers to spend a good portion of their lives overseas, even during the formative years. The SAR's well-publicised shortage of places at all educational levels, kindergarten through university, forces many families to send their children abroad; indeed, this is almost a Hong Kong rite of passage, a defining interval in local lives.

Pedigree is another form of identity as it pertains to the young, as Peter Phillips shows us in 'The Troubled Boyhood of Baldwin Wong'. From its rather brilliant opening line, *There are generations in all great bloodlines to whom genetics are not kind*, things only seem to go from bad to worse to almost comical for the title character, a poor little rich boy whose life is planned out for him more or less from the moment he leaves the womb. The fact that he is, to be kind, less than handsome only adds to the complications and compounds the difficulties he faces. How will he fit in with the framework his parents have constructed for him—a set of business, marriage, and social obligations he would never have chosen for himself if he had been given a choice in the matter?

Identity manifests in death as it does in life, as we see in Jenn Chan Lyman's 'The Seventh Year' and Ysabelle Cheung's 'Field, Burning'. Funerary traditions in Hong Kong are at the heart of 'The Seventh Year', in which a ritual disinterment goes wrong, and then worse than wrong, and then… curiously right. The narrator of this story identifies herself as a *zuk sing mui*, or *bamboo-stem girl, as in a hollow tube with walls on the inside that keep things from getting through*. Having left Hong Kong for the States at the age of five, she is keenly aware and repeatedly reminded upon her return—via Shanghai, where she lives with her Hongkonger husband—just how much she really belongs. And in 'Field, Burning', we take a look back in history as a grave-sweeper originally from Shandong province in China recounts the strange and horrifying tale of how she came to be a cemetery caretaker in Hong Kong more than a century after her birth. Can a (relatively) young man from hypermodern Hong Kong truly appreciate the extent to which his elders and their elders suffered in China's (relatively) recent history? After all, Hong Kong—despite its gleaming office towers, its sleek new subway trains, and its overflowing shopping malls—is never far from a rural Chinese past replete with ghosts, rituals, and other forms of superstition.

Several of the stories deal with the often uneasy relationships between expatriates, locals, and the wider Hong Kong Chinese culture. Stephanie Han deals with questions of identity and belonging in 'Swimming in Hong Kong' by telling a story from two viewpoints: that of Ruth, a 40-year-old African-American woman who is running out of patience with her inappropriate boss, and that of Froggy, a retired Hong Kong Chinese man. These two become acquainted at a public swimming pool where Ruth is training for a triathlon. Despite barriers of age, race, and nationality, the two strike up a sort of friendship—one that feels genuine and not transactional, despite its transience.

In 'Neville's Painting', Jason Ng passes judgment (or does he?) upon a Western attorney who revels in his contempt for his Chinese subordinates. Ng further allows us to bask for a moment in the current era's lack of sympathy for the woes of the one percent. It is always worthwhile to ask how much trouble these people bring upon themselves merely by existing and rather delightful to see them suffer. What's more, Ng draws upon a long tradition of stories in which arrogant Westerners mistake the accommodating, harmony-seeking aspects of Asian cultures for weakness. Things rarely end well for them. Will Ng's title character find redemption or meet the comeuppance he may deserve?

'Saving Grace' by Ploy Pirapokin follows the night-time exploits of three international school students, teenagers from well-off families whose parents would be shocked to know about their children's drug-dealing and petty-crime habits. The question of identity emerges in the disconnect between who these young people are and what is expected of them, and what they really do when they go out at night. How much of their earnest if not entirely convincing rebellion is to do with their affluence, and how much of it comes from merely being who they are, the beneficiaries of a shared, sheltered identity?

Hong Kong regards itself as an international city, yet it is both deeply and superficially Cantonese Chinese, and this is not an oxymoron. Even Chinese identity is not a one-dimensional construct, the Chinese nation being an assemblage of dozens of ethnicities, cultures, and languages. Mandarin (or *Putonghua*, as Beijing would like us to call it) attempts to unite the Chinese people, yet as we can see, what unity there is stops at the fenced and heavily guarded border between Hong Kong and Shenzhen. The territory's British colonial history, the official status of English, and the legacy Commonwealth legal system sets Hong Kong apart, as do its Handover—and SARs—related diaspora and its almost overwhelming mix of cultures. Even Hong Kong's novel geography, with the main island across a narrow harbour from the most crowded peninsula in the world, Kowloon, has resulted in the city being not quite like other places. If one looks closely at many of the issues the people and government of Hong Kong struggle with, one will see how much of this question really boils down to status. Who is a Hong Kong people and who isn't, and what does that mean? This book makes no attempt to present answers. The conversation is not only playing itself out on the streets, in the courts, and in the Legislative Council chambers; it's also capturing the attention of an emerging circle of authors.

[Marshall Moore]

## Why is this short fiction from Hong Kong in English?

If Hong Kong has a 'mother tongue', it certainly isn't English. Which begs the question as to why this anthology (or any anthology of literature or fiction from and of Hong Kong in English) can and should exist at all. We do not expect fiction from China to be in English, any more than we would expect American or British fiction to be in anything but English. But here we are, writing in English, and claiming an origin (after a fashion) of and from Hong Kong.

This is not the first anthology of English-language literary work in general or fiction specifically from Hong Kong. It is certainly not the first anthology of same that I've edited or co-edited. As a 'native daughter' of this city, and a fiction writer in English, it has been my fate (some might say, misfortune) to advocate for and pioneer what is a linguistically minority literature of a territory or region. Once we were British and now we are Chinese. Meanwhile, our fiction writers are a hybrid (some might say, mongrel) bunch of fitting misfits, all in possession of that curious sense of belonging conferred by the HKID, or Hong Kong Identity Card, permanent or otherwise, with its bureaucratic hierarchy of 'right of abode'. Yet when we set out to compile this anthology—'we' being two fiction writers and editors with our own curious connections to this city—we never once considered national or ethnic exclusivity, the way editors of an anthology of, say, Singaporean or Indian or Filipino fiction might, and the way so many literary prizes do. The only two criteria that mattered to us were language and quality: the work had to be short fiction written in English and it had to compel our imagination. The original linguistic umbrella of World Englishes was, mercifully, set aside: there is virtually no 'Hong Kong English' to speak of that informs, in any significant way, the stories included in this volume.

When *City Voices: Hong Kong Writing in English 1945 to the Present* was issued,[7] it was the first anthology of previously published work to include fiction under the rubric of 'Hong Kong writing in English'. Fiction was by Western expatriate residents or the handful of overseas Chinese or part-Chinese writers with some kind of connection to the city. In other words, there were few authors that my co-editor and I could completely describe as 'local Hong Kong Chinese'. Similarly, in compiling the anthology *Fifty-Fifty: New Hong Kong Writing,*[8] published in 2008, it was difficult to find much fiction by local Hong Kong Chinese writers. In fact, fiction was the smallest category of submissions received to the open call.

Today, the majority of fiction in English from this city that in some way can be considered 'local' is still by expatriates, resident non-Chinese nationals, or Chinese 'astronauts' of one kind of

---

[7] *City Voices: Hong Kong Writing in English from 1945 to the Present*, ed. Xu Xi and Mike Ingham (Hong Kong: Hong Kong University Press, 2003).
[8] *Fifty-Fifty: New Hong Kong writing*, ed. Xu Xi (Hong Kong: Haven Books, 2008).

another, meaning that their lives are split between Hong Kong and someplace else, usually an English-speaking country.

Yet in compiling this anthology, we noted a new voice emerging by younger writers who are perhaps more local or 'native' to this city, despite their lives abroad. For one thing, they are very much at home in Hong Kong. These are the TCKs, third-culture kids, whose passports, ethnicities, cultures, and lives are global, cosmopolitan in the way the philosopher Kwame Anthony Appiah has described it, but with a strong local connection that is deep-rooted and real. It is a globalised culture with a specific local face: as much as it might have in common with the TCK culture from Paris or New York or Dubai, it has its own uniquely Hong Kong spirit and feel. English is for this group of writers the natural (sometimes the only) language for fiction, and its linguistic parent is British or American or Canadian or Australian or a curious combination of all of the above, because it is an English born out of international schools and universities. When they locate their characters in today's Hong Kong, they do not describe the city the way foreign writers are often inclined to, with that explanatory overlay for the Western reader. Hong Kong *is* the world as they know it, with no apologies to London or New York or the rest of that dominant literary English fictional world.

Will this mean a growth in the local English language fiction from this city? Perhaps. As the founder and director of Asia's first international, low-residency MFA (Master of Fine Arts) Creative Writing programme in English, housed in a local university, I have met an increasing number of young writers from the city who can or will write only in English, even if Chinese (or another language) is their mother tongue. They speak with many accents—the obvious ones being British and North American, but equally these days, Singaporean or Australian or Filipino or even South American. Likewise, as this anthology attests, there is new breed of alphabet soup Chinese writer: no one is a 'pure' ABC[2], BBC, CBC, etc. anymore, meaning the American- or Australian-born Chinese, British-born or Canadian-born, etc. who fits comfortably into the Asian-American literary tradition of immigrant fiction. The writers who can be so classified are as at home in Hong Kong as they are in Los

Angeles. Even the non-Chinese resident or expatriate writers in this volume are much more a part of local society, and the stories they write demonstrate that. In fact, the fictions by such writers were the more compelling submissions we received; 'post-colonial' does really mean that the colonial or foreign perspective in contemporary Hong Kong fiction feels dated, clichéd, and out of step with the current global, trans-cultural reality.

Much of this has to do with China's ascent as a major economic force and Hong Kong's curious position as China's 'international' city with its odd, non-Communist history and reality. This has brought a new kind of expatriate to Hong Kong. While a significant number are still comparable to the original colonial expatriate—economically privileged, segregated from local life, uninterested in local culture—the more significant growth has been in middle-class, ordinary professionals of all stripes who come armed with a fluency in Mandarin (and even Cantonese in some cases); an eagerness to participate; a genuine interest in Hong Kong's sophisticated, global, city-of-opportunity culture; and the willingness and desire to observe the city from within, on its own terms. This perspective informs the fiction they write. Some leave, others stay and call the city home, and their offspring are that curious generation of TCKs who are decidedly at home here, regardless of where their parents are from. And while many TCKs will continue down the road of Hong Kong's pragmatic culture and become doctors, lawyers, Chinese chiefs, some will and do find their way into the literary arts.

In other words, the possibility for a literary culture, in English, has a hope for at least a modest future.

*

Fiction happens when the facts alone fail fully to give voice to the human condition as the writer experiences it. It is a form of truth-seeking, and is the result of an imaginative leap of faith. For Hong Kong English-language fiction to take that leap, the writer must be confident that the English language can and will give voice to what needs to be told. Our British colonial overlords bequeathed us a language (which till the mid-'70s was the city's only official language) that has, over time, been bastardised, Sinicised, globalised, and transformed into one of three 'official' languages of this city, alongside Cantonese and Mandarin, under our Chinese overlords. Yet English in this city is, for the most part, a pragmatic language, one to learn because you must, for commerce and connection to the world; the 'real' culture of this city is still very, very Chinese. To write fiction in English of Hong Kong forces you to confront the validity of English as such a voice.

Yet the imagination is a curious thing. *What good is a book without pictures,* Alice wondered, just as we might ask, *what good is an 'official language' if it's limited in what it can be used for?* When confronted by the language of the Jabberwocky, *'And the wabe is the grass plot around the sun dial, I suppose?' said Alice, surprised at her own ingenuity.* The answer to her question is expansive, one that reassures those of us who do not succumb to unnecessary limits: *'Of course it is. It's called "wabe", you know, because it goes a long way before it, and a long way behind it—'*

So here is this anthology of Hong Kong short fiction, in English. Go *gyre and gimble in the wabe.* It might surprise you.

[Xu Xi]

# MAKE-BELIEVE
Yeung Chak Yan

Kate met the boy for the first time at the herbal tea shop yesterday. He introduced himself as her older brother.

He is eight.

She is thrice his age.

He did not seem to understand what the problem was. He simply shrugged and told her he was called Danny too.

When Danny died, the boy probably had not even been born yet.

'It was on the same day,' her mother later said, as if that explained everything.

'So?' said Kate. 'It was a coincidence, of course.'

And an unpleasant one, too. But as always, her mother does not agree.

Reincarnation. That is what her mother believes. Her mother, who has stayed strong after her father died, who started up a company all on her own and single-handedly supported the whole family, is somehow now convinced that the eight-year-old boy is Danny reborn. He knew too much, she said. He acted just like Danny. They even shared the same favourite food. It was no coincidence.

'No, it's no coincidence,' Kate conceded. 'It's a fraud.'

The more she listened, the clearer it became, and yet her mother refused to see the obvious.

Apparently, she had been taking care of 'Danny' for almost a year already. Every day at three, she would wait for him at the school gate and drive him to Central for after-school tutorial classes—not because he was struggling with his schoolwork, she insisted, but all children attended extra classes these days, and it would not do for him to be left behind. His classes begin at four, so they would have a drink at a nearby herbal-tea shop first, and the boy would start on his homework. He would then stay at the learning centre until eight at night, and his real mother would come and take him home. It is, Kate was told, the best arrangement for the two families—the boy's parents needed to work in the day and Kate's mother, being the head of her company, could afford a more flexible schedule.

'You don't have to see him again if you don't want to,' her mother added. 'You're only staying here for a short while. I'm sure there are places you want to visit.'

Kate still remembers the last time she returned to Hong Kong and how her mother was reluctant even to let her visit her friends because that would mean less time for them to spend together. Now, all her mother cares about is to make sure 'Danny' gets to his tutorial classes on time.

'Dinner's ready, Kate!'

'Coming, Mum,' she calls back and pushes herself off the bed.

With her opened suitcase on the floor, the room seems even smaller than usual and she almost trips when she makes her way to the door. After years of living in Bristol, it is hard to imagine how she managed to share this tiny space with Danny when they were young. She never complained, never even craved a space of her own. It was only when Danny was gone that the room became unbearable, especially since her mother would not let her put her brother's belongings away. Even now, the upper bunk of their beds was kept clean. His old clothes were in the wardrobe and the right side of the bookshelf was still filled with his books. It hurt to be in here, but these painful reminders seemed to comfort her mother, as if, by preserving the room, she could trick herself into believing that Danny has only gone for a long trip and would return one day.

And he did return, or so her mother claimed.

'Kate?'

'On my way!'

She pushes a chair aside and leaves the room that holds too many memories. She wonders if the boy has ever been in here. It's likely. Her mother has already invited him 'home' for dinner a few times, after all, and it is too easy to imagine him running around on bare feet, climbing onto Danny's bed, and claiming the space as his own.

But there is no such thing as reincarnation.

Kate is staying in Hong Kong for two weeks this time. Not too long, but there is still plenty of time for her to get to the bottom of this ridiculous charade and drag her mother out of it.

*

Lyndhurst Terrace has become unrecognizable. The Pizza Express, with its bright-blue signboards and large plate-glass windows, used to stand out among the old stores. Not anymore. The stores have been replaced by cafés and oyster bars and brightly-lit shops selling overpriced cooking utensils, organic products, and essential oils, clearly aimed at Westerners. Even the bakery she frequented has moved, and it is supposed to be a famous one since the last governor Patten loved its egg tarts. The new location is only a few blocks away, but the egg tarts taste different now, likely because of the fame, or perhaps because Danny is no longer here. When they were small, he always saved the larger half for her, but then they grew older and half a tart was no longer quite enough. He started buying two then, one for her, one for himself, usually just before dinnertime. They never told their mother. It was their little secret.

She walks past the bakery and turns into Hollywood Road. The old herbal-tea shop comes into view. It is a small one with only a few tables, though most people prefer to take their drinks away or finish them at the entrance. It is one of the few stores that still manage to survive. The boy is there, as expected, talking with her mother.

Kate ran into them at the same time and place a few days ago, but it was not entirely by accident. Back when they lived in Lyndhurst Terrace, Danny and she had spent a considerable portion of their pocket money at this shop. It was near their old primary school, and on a scorching summer day a cup of cold sugarcane juice was the next best thing to Coke, which was forbidden. Danny, though, always ordered the hot one. He claimed the heat made the sugarcane taste sweeter.

The boy said the same.

It had to be an act. But how did he know?

She orders a cup of cold sugarcane juice and takes the seat opposite the boy, who regards her with a flat gaze. He is in his school uniform, and his white shirt seems too large on his tiny frame.

'Sis,' he says.

'I am not your sister.'

His calmness unnerves her. It is simply not natural. But this maturity can be explained, can't it? Her mother said the boy has been 'remembering'.

Remembering about being Danny.

Of course, he is called Danny too, but a name means nothing. There are lots of Dannys in Hong Kong. Not as many as Kelvins or Michaels, but still.

Her mother shifts in her seat. 'What are you doing here, Kate?'

'Can't I come and see you? I'll be leaving Hong Kong soon.'

'Of course, dear.'

The long silence that follows is worse than the forced smile on her mother's face—and likely on her own too—but she can't think of anything to say. Her mother is clearly not interested in where she has been this morning, nor in how she almost got lost in Causeway Bay because the place has changed too much. No, her mother only wants to spend time with the boy. Just like before, back when Danny was still alive. He was the favoured one, not Kate. Never Kate.

'It's done, Mum,' says the boy, breaking the silence.

And in an instant, the fake smile becomes real.

'Really? Let me see.'

Kate watches as her mother flips through the boy's notebook and praises his good work. Her voice is gentle and caring, one Kate does not remember ever hearing before. Still, she stays where she is. The boy is the intruder, not her.

*

A week before she has to leave, her mother is down with the 'flu but refuses to let Kate take the boy to tutorial classes for her. It is only when Kate says that 'flu is contagious that she relents at last. The boy says nothing after hearing his usual caretaker is sick.

Kate does not have a driver's licence in Hong Kong, so they take the bus to Central instead. The boy drags his feet as they walk to the herbal-tea shop. His forehead is wet with sweat, and the heavy school bag on his back bends him over, but still he insists on having a cup of hot sugarcane juice.

'Are you sure don't want the cold one?' asks Kate.

He shakes his head.

'Even Danny drinks the cold one at times, you know.'

He peers up at her. Had this been any other kid, the suspicion on his face would have been cute.

'The hot one is fine,' he murmurs, lowering his head again.

He is a smart one, but still a child, and his reaction alone has exposed him—he has been mimicking instead of 'remembering'. But why? What is he trying to accomplish?

Kate sits opposite him again and watches him do his mathematics homework. He has forgotten to do multiplication first before adding the numbers together.

'The first step is already wrong,' she says.

He looks up from his notebook and frowns.

Instead of pointing out his mistake, she finds herself thinking of her mother and the way she smiled at the boy. In the end, all she manages to say is, 'Danny would have no problem finishing this.'

The boy blushes and looks away. 'I don't remember everything.'

And of course, this is the best explanation for every inconsistency, isn't it? He does not remember everything, so a slip or two is to be expected. But his act is already falling apart, and it's still six days before Kate has to leave.

*

She buys him a cup of cold sugarcane juice the next day and tells him to try it before he can open his mouth.

'How is it?' she asks.

He shrugs.

21

'Better, isn't it?'

He ignores her and continues to do his homework, copying a passage of his textbook word for word. It is a story of the Yellow River, about how it has given birth to a great nation, and how her 'sons' and 'daughters' should be proud of their heritage and love their 'mother country'. Having grown up in colonial Hong Kong, Kate finds the bold patriotism disgusting. Love cannot be taught or transferred, only earned.

The boy writes each stroke slowly, as if he is carving an art piece, making sure each Chinese character falls within the pale blue grid of his notebook. Kate used to write that way too, as did Danny, because their mother demanded that their calligraphy— and everything else—be perfect. And before they realised it, her standard had become their own and the pressure that came with it had ended up costing Danny his life.

The boy lets out a low grunt and scrubs the paper with his eraser because the ending tip of a stroke is too long. Kate leans back and watches him write, erasing his words again and again until not a line is out of place. She wonders if he understands what he is copying.

\*

The next day, the boy refuses the cup of cold sugarcane juice, so he goes without a drink. He is doing mathematics again, though he keeps glancing at her. They sit for half an hour and he manages to get only two questions done.

'What is it?' asks Kate.

'Nothing.' He bends further down so his hair covers his face.

'Do you need help?'

He shakes his head, his hand tightening around his pencil. 'He wouldn't have needed help… right?'

'No, but you aren't him, are you? You're only eight.'

He looks up briefly and lowers his head again. 'Everyone wants me to be him.' He fiddles with his pen. 'Even the teachers like me more when I act like him.'

Of course, Danny was a model student, always polite and working hard all the time.

'I don't want you to be him,' says Kate. 'I want you to be yourself.'

He wrinkles his nose. 'Yeah, I know.'

They sit in silence, then he reaches for the cup of sugarcane juice and drinks half of it in one go—he must be thirsty. He leaves his bite mark on the straw. Danny would never do that.

'Who told you to lie?' asks Kate.

The boy shrugs and takes another long sip of his drink.

'Answer me.'

He ignores her and picks up his pen again, but makes no move to continue doing his homework. He starts squirming after some time.

'Ma told me to,' he mumbles.

'Your mother. Why?'

'Said everyone had to earn for themselves.'

So it is about money. Not surprising. This is Hong Kong, after all. But the fact that a child is involved makes Kate wonder just how low the people of her hometown have fallen.

*

She calls the boy's mother that afternoon, and they meet in the McDonald's near the learning centre, just the two of them. Lai looks to be in her forties. Her skin is pale like the boy's and she looks tired, but there is a sharpness in her eyes that puts Kate on edge.

'Danny was an accident. We couldn't afford another child,' says Lai, cutting straight to the point. 'We tried to, at first, but then my husband lost his legs in an accident and everything went downhill. I'm working ten hours a day now, but I can barely earn enough to pay the rent. Jeff—my older son—went to the same school as your brother, and they were in the same club. Chess, I believe. He was upset for weeks after the news of what happened reached the school and wouldn't stop talking about how much your brother had taught him. Then one day, he started to call the new baby Danny.'

'You mean he believed—'

'I don't know what he believed, but Jeff was only thirteen then

23

and Danny was born on the same day your brother committed suicide. It helped him cope, somehow.'

'And now you are short on money, so you decided to use a mere coincidence to make my mother raise your son for you,' says Kate. 'Do you have any idea what you're doing to her?'

'Do you honestly think your mother doesn't know what's going on?' says Lai. 'She knows and she doesn't care. All she wants is to have her son back.'

Lai is being awfully open, as if she knows there is nothing Kate can do to change her mother's mind. And it is true, isn't it? Deep down, Kate has always known that there is nothing to be exposed and no one to be convinced. Her mother would never be fooled by something so obvious and has to have known about the boy's act. No, she is a part of the boy's act, and the boy a part of hers.

'This isn't a game of make-believe,' says Kate.

'No, this is an exchange,' says Lai. 'Raising a child is expensive, Miss Chow. I don't want Danny to grow up and blame me for not doing what's best for him.'

Kate shakes her head. 'You're forcing him to act like someone he isn't. How can this be the best for him?'

'He can afford new books and uniforms now. And if he ever wants to study abroad like you did, he can have that option. I don't have much education myself, Miss Chow, but I know money buys opportunities.'

There is nothing Kate can say to counter that point. 'What about my mother? How is this the best for her?'

'We have talked a few times, your mother and I,' says Lai. 'I know she supported you to study in England and paid for all your expenses, but then you refused to return to Hong Kong and left her alone.'

Kate tenses. 'I don't believe this is your business.'

'Do you know your mother thinks you are punishing her? And that she thinks she deserves it? Even now, she is blaming herself for your brother's death. That is why she lets you do whatever you want.' Lai pauses. 'But it has been years, Miss Chow. It is time for you to stop taking advantage of your brother's death and start being a responsible daughter.'

Kate wants to deny the outrageous accusation, but for a

moment she finds herself unable to speak. Her chair suddenly seems hard and uncomfortable, and the noise around them unbearably loud.

'You gladly accepted your mother's money and left to start a life of your own,' Lai continues. 'You know she has no one besides you, but you hardly ever come back to visit her.' She leans forward. 'If I don't know better, Miss Chow, I would say you want to see your mother miserable.'

'That's not true,' Kate hears herself saying.

'Then prove it,' says Lai. 'You have moved on, so why won't you let your mother do the same? She has found someone to take care of again and she is happy. Are you going to take this away from her? After all she has done for you?'

\*

The day before she has to leave, she takes the boy to the Seven-Eleven and buys him a can of coke. He is much more talkative this time, telling her about his day at school and his teachers. He also stops calling her 'Sis'. They stay at a nearby park for a while, then she takes him to the bakery and buys two egg tarts, one for him, one for herself.

'How does it taste?' she asks.

'I like it.'

The smile on his face is painful to look at.

'It used to taste better, but this is not half bad,' she says. 'Danny liked it, so... I guess you would too.'

He stiffens, then his face falls. He stares at her for a while longer, as if hoping she would change her mind, and looks away, bending his head low so that his hair once again obscures his features.

Kate tells herself that it is for the best. Her mother will be happy. And one day, surely, the boy will be too, once he understands what this little make-believe has brought him. Yes, it is for the best.

# THE SEVENTH YEAR
Jenn Chan Lyman

When Edwin said one morning over breakfast that he had to go home to sort out Helena's bones, the first image that came to mind was my husband standing in a grave, waving a femur in the air, sporting waders like a fly fisherman. He had to be joking, obviously. I'd never heard the Cantonese phrase he used, and frankly, it sounded obscene: *zap gwat*, *zap* literally meaning *to sort out or pick up*, and *gwat* meaning *bones*. Edwin has always had a dark sense of humour. He likes to tease me with urban myths about human meat buns and haunted hospitals, to 'steel my delicate American nerves,' so he says. But it wasn't like him to joke about his late wife. I looked up from the article I was proofing, a forkful of scrambled eggs suspended *en route* to my mouth. He was facing me, elbows astride an already empty plate, hands folded beneath his chin, looking serious. We were in the breakfast nook of our kitchen, surrounded by the smell of fried bacon (ours) mixed with the scent of fried garlic and dough (the neighbours'). I could hear Mr and Mrs Lu in the small lane below chattering incomprehensibly in Shanghainese. A cheerful glow from the window above the kitchen sink bathed the table and my strange, serious husband, in a soft lemony haze. There was a sharpness in his eyes that usually preceded something big, like that Sunday two years ago when he'd announced that his company was promoting him on the condition that we move from Hong Kong to Shanghai immediately, or that night three years ago when he'd taken my hands into his and asked me oh-so-solemnly if I, Connie May Kay Lam, would be his wife. Something was definitely up. I set down my fork, bummed that my eggs would be cold in a second, and waited.

'I'm sorry, hon, you probably don't even know what I'm talking about. *Zap gwat* sounds weird, doesn't it, my *zuk sing mui*,' he said in a mix of Cantonese and English, touching me under the chin with two fingers. When anybody else called me *zuk sing* I bristled, but not when Edwin did. He said it like it was a cherished characteristic, rather than a cultural embarrassment. I left Hong Kong for the States when I was five years old, early enough to qualify me as a *zuk sing mui*, or bamboo-stem girl, as in a hollow tube with walls on the inside that keep things from getting through. Things like *zap gwat*. Since the day I moved back to Hong Kong after college, I've been reminded all too often of how *zuk sing* I really am. This was one of those times. I blushed.

Edwin moved his plate to the side and folded his arms back into an A-frame under his chin. 'In Hong Kong, with certain public cemeteries, people are only allowed to remain in the ground for six to ten years. To, you know, make room for others. So, for Helena, it's the seventh year.'

I focused on maintaining a neutral expression, something I always did when anything Helena-related came up. Which was almost never. Edwin was not much of a talker when it came to most things, but especially when it came to Helena. I met him three years after she died. All I knew from the bits and pieces gleaned from his friends and relatives over the years was that Edwin and Helena met in Form 1, stayed in touch even after Edwin moved to Toronto at fifteen, and married as soon as Edwin moved back to Hong Kong a few years after college. It was one of those perfect high-school-sweetheart romances that made you want to gag. Not to mention, this Helena had been one of those annoyingly beautiful girls. Opalescent skin like an elven princess in *Lord of the Rings*. An Asian Arwen. Except tinier and more petite than Liv Tyler. I don't remember which of his tactful cousins told me that. Most likely Boris, the Tolkien nut.

I saw a picture of Helena once at my in-laws and tried ever since to forget her pretty little face. So the fact that Edwin wasn't much of a sharer didn't bother me. Who wants to be reminded of the late wife, anyway? He was open about everything else in his life when I asked, unlike some other guys I'd dated, and I figured, everyone deserves to take one mystery to the grave. The important thing was that when I met him he seemed ready to move past his tragedy and I wasn't going to let a dead wife be the deal-breaker, not with him anyway. By the time I'd even heard of Helena, I was already up to my eyebrows in love with this serious, quirky man with his thoughtful looks, gentle manners, and phenomenal collection of Super 8 silent films. I swept the late wife to the back of my mind like a previous dalliance with drugs, or a stalker ex-girlfriend: all in the past. And anyway, death and dying was the kind of talk that made me green. Even that morning, as I tried to absorb what he was saying, I could feel eggs, milk, and bacon squelching in my stomach. *Make room for others?* Presumably other *corpses.* Gross.

'So I have to go back, in two weeks or so. Help her parents move her. They probably got the notice from the cemetery a couple months ago, but forgot to tell me until last week.'

I could feel my face twitching and barely managed to maintain control. Last week? Which meant that he'd waited a whole week to tell me. Hmm. And what in the world did he mean by 'move her'? Move her where? For a second, the leftover eggs on my fork looked like they were alive and quivering, and the image of Edwin in waders was getting less and less amusing.

'I was thinking maybe you could come with me?'

'What about work?' I said, regretting the words as soon as they came out. Jesus. How insensitive could I be? If he was willing to go all the way back to Hong Kong for a weekend, it must be important. I opened my mouth to say something redeeming but he was already responding.

'It'd be on a Saturday, we'd be back in time for Monday. No time off.'

I paused for a second, but of course, there was really no acceptable answer other than: 'Okay, yeah sure. I mean, of course.'

'Is it too weird?'

I looked up at him. His forehead above his strong, straight nose was creased with concern. He had one of those memorable faces: high cheekbones; smooth, tanned skin. I'd noticed him right away when he'd first walked into that Chamber of Commerce brunch years ago. He wasn't very tall, but solid and athletically built, with a chest that filled out his dress shirts well. Even though the web design company he worked for was more casual than business casual, as creative director he made it a point to wear a shirt and tie Mondays through Thursdays, a habit I found adorable. He was wearing one of his many banker-blue shirts that morning, and his tie was swept over his shoulder to avoid grease splatters from the stove. Part of me wanted to ask if he was okay, if this sudden trip back home stirred up sad, dark memories, but the rest of me was afraid to confirm what I'd thought were defunct suspicions that he still thought about her, the other wife, not 'ex' by choice but by fate. My heart clenched. How could he not be sad? I scooted my chair toward him, pulled his tie from over his shoulder, and ironed it flat against his chest with the palm of my hand. It was time for me to buck up, be the good wife.

'No, it's fine. I want to be there. It's good to go together.'

He kissed me on the forehead and said, 'I thought so, too.'

Over the next few days, Edwin made arrangements for the weekend after next. It would be a quick trip, no time to see old friends. The logistics were as follows: Saturday morning, fly back and head to his parents' place. Saturday night, dinner with Helena's family. Sunday morning, go to the cemetery, where Helena's grave would be exhumed and her coffin removed, her bones retrieved, dusted, and deposited into a bone urn, which would then be interred in the columbarium on site. (Yes, they would be present for the entire ritual, but don't worry, it would be quick and easy, nothing too grisly, they do this kind of thing in front of families all the time.) Then Sunday night, free at last to catch the last flight home.

I knew that Edwin's presence was not mandatory, but out of respect. I understood this. I appreciated his role in it, his sense of duty. But even though his actions betrayed nothing beyond duty, the whole idea was unsettling, insidious like midsummer mould edging under my skin as the dreaded weekend approached.

The week leading up to the trip, I couldn't sleep much at all. I crouched under the covers, pretending to sleep, eyes smarting from the bright screen of my iPhone as I stumbled through articles in Chinese that described the removal process. My head filled with images of bone specialists cracking open coffin covers, rotting flesh still clinging to bone, and brass urns housing skeletons coaxed into foetal positions. While Edwin slept soundly beside me, I scoured and pored, steeling my delicate American nerves for the bizarro weekend ahead.

*

On the prescribed Saturday, we arrived in Hong Kong an hour and a half late. Although Shanghai's Pudong Airport was even more modern than Hong Kong International and just as packed with travellers, as we joined the rush of bodies and trolley suitcases I couldn't help but notice an inherent order in the way people moved in Hong Kong, stepping efficiently around and beside other bodies rather than over and into them. The air felt more oxygenated, crisp with Cantonese, rather than a muggy blend of Mandarin and Shanghainese. Relaxing my grip on the handle of my suitcase, I took in the familiar scent of the airport, which reminded me of the way my dad's suitcase used to smell after his trips to Hong Kong when I was a kid, that massive leather case filled to bursting with various mundane items Mom was homesick for, like white flower oil and mentholated Tempo tissue packets. She would take out a tissue and press it to my nose, and as the menthol tickled my nostrils she would say, 'That's what home smells like.' I inhaled deeply and there it was, whether in the surrounding air or my imagination: mentholated Tempos. I smiled. Even under the circumstances, it was good to be back. Edwin reached for my free hand and led us through the crowds.

By the time we tumbled out of the cab in North Point, it was two in the afternoon. Edwin's parents, the Laus, lived in one of twenty-six blocks that made up a massive apartment complex situated above a labyrinthine indoor mall, which in turn straddled a subway station that yawned deep underground. In Hong Kong, it seemed that no matter where you stood, there were people around, above, and below you. Space was the city's hottest commodity: an inch of gold for a foot of soil, my dad would say. I peered up at the crown of buildings as we crossed through the courtyard towards Block P, and suddenly thought of Helena in the ground. Jesus. Even the dead fought over real estate in this city. Move over already, it's my turn to decompose. A photo from my research materialised in my head: a bone specialist, masked and gloved, painting an ulna red. Or was it a humerus? I shuddered.

When we emerged from the elevator on the thirty-second floor, Edwin's parents were waiting in their doorway, having been buzzed by the doorman. Edwin's mom was wearing one of her customary outfits: linen capris and a jaunty chiffon blouse. Jade bangles glistened on both wrists. The only thing sunnier than her blouse and accessories was the broad smile on her face. Edwin's dad towered over her from behind. He was a lean man with a serene, oval face that reminded me of this animated pencil in a cartoon I used to watch. Precise Pencil, the sheriff of a town populated with everything a kid could want in a pencil case: Ornery Eraser, Cheerful Chalk, No-Nonsense Ballpoint, Crazy Crayon, Trouble-Maker Marker. Precise Pencil was the one who maintained order, kept everyone on the straight and narrow, just like my father-in-law, who had worked at the Inland Revenue Department his entire career and recently retired at sixty-five. The kind of guy who ordered whiskey neat and never got drunk. He stood there in a charcoal-grey collared shirt and black slacks, a perfect contrast to his polychromatic wife. Cantonese families aren't big on hugs, but I've always thought that if I ever did hug my father-in-law, he would smell like a freshly sharpened pencil.

'*Lou-je, Naai-naai,*' I said. Father-in-law, Mother-in-law.

'Come in, come in. You two must be hungry. I'm re-warming the soup now,' said Naai-naai, reaching out for our bags, but Lou-je got to me first, relieving me of my suitcase and ushering me, then Edwin, inside. The flat was filled with the aroma of minced-meat eggplant and pickled-vegetable omelette, Edwin's favourite dishes. My stomach grumbled.

'Did you guys wait for us?' Edwin asked, pulling the door closed behind him. 'You should have eaten first, no use for all four of us to starve.'

'Nah, we had a big breakfast,' Naai-naai said, calling from the kitchen. 'Sit down, sit down. But wash your hands first.'

The flat was small compared to our flat in Shanghai, but at nine hundred square feet, it was considered large by Hong Kong standards. There were three bedrooms, two bathrooms, living room, dining room, kitchen, and maid's room, all packed together in a tight formation of squares and rectangles. The hall bathroom was so small that a person could wash his hands while still sitting on the toilet. I stared at the bathroom mirror, rubbing the brown smudge under my left eye where my eyeliner had run, and thought, *Shanghai isn't so bad. At least there's space.* Our old flat in Hong Kong had only been two-thirds the size of this one. How we'd managed to fit all our stuff in a six-hundred-square-foot apartment was beyond me. '*Sanpouzai! Sik faan lah!*' Naai-naai's voice cut through the thin door. Time to eat.

My bowl of rice was already topped with minced-meat eggplant when I sat down at the table. Naai-naai was her boisterous self, chatting about Sixth Uncle's hip surgery (successful), the neighbours' new Shih Tzu (disturbing the peace), Edwin's brother Joseph's new girlfriend in Toronto (Vietnamese... or something like that), and their recent trip to a spa in Shenzhen (delightful). She was more dogged than usual, bounding from one topic to another without so much as a breath in between. After the dishes were cleared and the oranges brought out, Lou-je finally interrupted her flow, his tone soft but insistent.

'Everything prepared for tomorrow?' he said, pulling strands of pith from the orange in his hand and setting them in a neat pile on the edge of his placemat.

Even though the question was not directed at her, Naai-naai's face flushed and clouded at the same time. I reached for an orange, despite having declined one a second ago.

'Should be.' Edwin replied. He was creating a similar pile of pith on his own placemat that suggested a certain male-Lau obsession with the orange in its barest state.

'You're meeting them tonight?'

'Yes.'

'Dinner seems unnecessary.'

'Mm.'

'Maybe Connie should stay here for dinner instead.'

At this, Naai-naai re-animated and said, 'I already bought bird's nest and fish maw. Good for women. *Sanpouzai* should stay here with us tonight.'

'I already told them she's coming.' Another spongy white strand joined the pile.

'Son, it's good of you to go, but Connie doesn't need to.' Lou-je set his naked orange down and wiped his hands carefully, first the right, then the left.

I was confused. I'd never seen the Laus so tense. They were usually easygoing and amiable, unlike my own family, who talked over each other and broke out into little tiffs over nothing. I stuffed a pithy section into my mouth and chewed as quietly as possible.

'Don't worry, *Lou-dau*, it's going to be fine. Her mother specifically invited Connie. It would be rude.'

'Those people don't deserve tact—' Naai-naai said sharply, before Lou-je cut her off by placing his hand on top of hers.

We ate our respective oranges in silence. I'd expected things to be awkward, but with Helena's family, not with my in-laws. What did Naai-naai mean by 'those people'? It was all very weird. Edwin stood up first to clear the table and I followed, hoping we would have a moment alone so that I could ask him what the hell was going on, but Naai-naai and Lou-je were close behind. We bustled about in the kitchen until Naai-naai finally shooed us all out, demanding in a blithe voice that we head downstairs to walk off lunch.

After the walk, the four of us were lured into the shopping mall by a cluster of sale signs, and Edwin and I didn't have a moment alone until the mini-bus ride on the way to dinner with Helena's family, the Pangs. But with the traffic bleating all around and the breakneck speed at which we were travelling, we spoke little and held onto our seats.

The moment I stepped into the private room of the Chinese restaurant the Pangs had chosen, I knew that I was in for a fun-filled night. Four pairs of eyes were staring at me. The father and the sister (presumably, since her features were a faded facsimile of Helena's) had the same cold, lethal expression, while the mother and the dog (a Jack Russell terrier in a pink crocheted vest with matching booties and bow) exuded mild curiosity, *sans* venom. The mother greeted Edwin and nodded at me; the father, without a word or glance, gestured for us to sit down. The two empty seats left were between the dog and the mother; I chose the dog. As soon as I sat down, the dog stood up on all fours and began yapping at me while the sister looked on, arms folded, the corners of her mouth twitching. Finally the mother picked up a piece of barbecued pork with her chopsticks and tossed it at the dog, missing my sleeve by an inch. The dog snapped the meat in its jaws and shut up.

Mrs Pang supplied the conversation with a calm litany of questions directed at Edwin. *How's Shanghai? How's the job? How are your parents? Is your brother married yet?* Relatively invisible, I glanced around the table, taking in each individual Pang. The mother, sitting to Edwin's left, reminded me of a hummingbird, with her small bones and quiet intensity. She had the air of a woman who'd been extraordinarily beautiful in her youth. Like Helena. I felt a small twinge under my sternum. The father was a large man with a tight, bulbous belly and a sour expression that seemed habitual. How in the world he'd landed the mother was beyond me. The sister, however, was the biggest surprise. Literally. She was huge, much larger than her mother and dangerously close to her father's girth. All of Helena's delicate features were bunched at the centre of her round face and the flab from her arms hung loosely as she tackled the crispy chicken with her fingers. Out of the corner of my eye, I watched her tear off the skin and, with some reluctance, pass the glistening scraps to the dog. I felt sorry for her. It was hard being the fat girl in the family. I'd gone through a chubby phase myself back in high school; even after the pounds disappear, the ridicule and self-loathing never go away, not completely anyway. It occurred to me then that I'd never told Edwin about my chubby phase. Funny how, after four years, there were still things in my past that he didn't know. Then, after the steamed fish had been picked clean, Mrs Pang rested her gaze on me and asked in slow, elementary Cantonese if I understood. It took me a second to swallow my mouthful of rice and mumble a response in Cantonese, 'Can understand.'

Mrs Pang lifted her tattooed indigo eyebrows. 'Oh, I thought you were a *zuk sing*. Good. We can all understand each other then. So what do you do in Shanghai?'

'I work in, um, corporate communications.'

'What's that?'

'We should talk about tomorrow,' the father interrupted, speaking for the first time that night. He had a high-pitched voice that didn't seem to fit a man of his size. 'We meet at nine in the morning at the front entrance. Wo Hip Cemetery. The specialist will be there at nine-thirty. There's paperwork, so don't be late.'

Edwin gave a respectful nod, to which Mr Pang responded with nothing but the same, stolid expression.

'If there's anything you'd like to put in the bone urn,' Mrs Pang began, but was cut off by the father, who glared at his wife and said, 'There's no need. We will bring what's necessary.'

'Well, if her husband has something he'd like to add, I think it's perfectly reasonable for—'

Mr Pang's face reddened as he replied. 'I will not tolerate it. His being here is already…' He paused for a moment, collecting himself, then continued evenly, 'You ask your own daughter's murderer to come, fine, because he is her husband under law, but don't ask me to tolerate anything more.'

I looked over at Edwin, who was grasping his teacup with both hands, his face twisted in an expression I'd never seen before. I couldn't tell if he was livid or mortified or what? Murderer? What the hell was going on? I wanted to inch over, grab his hand, touch his leg or something, but I couldn't move.

'Please don't talk that way,' Mrs Pang said through her teeth.

'Why not,' the sister interjected. 'Everyone knows he killed her. Let's not pretend otherwise.' The hairs rose all along my bare arms.

'That's enough. No one asked for your opinion,' Mrs Pang hissed at her daughter. 'He is her husband. She will be buried in the presence of her husband. That is all.' The last part she directed at Mr Pang, who sat sullen and obdurate, his belly even more distended than before.

Edwin stood up, trembling. 'Thank you for dinner. We will leave first. See you in the morning.'

He turned to pull out my chair and I shot up, almost losing my balance. The dog snapped at me and began to bark. Its vicious yapping tailed us down the hall as we left the restaurant.

Edwin finally spoke when we reached a quiet section of a pedestrian overpass on our way back to the minibus stop. He put his hand on the small of my back and I flinched, surprised by his touch. We'd been walking side by side insulated in our own thoughts, or in my case, shock.

'Hey,' he said, gently turning me by the shoulders to face him. A large family was walking toward us, young kids fanning out around their parents, waving pinwheels on long stems. We stepped toward the railing and out of the way.

'I'm so sorry, hon. How awful, to have to sit through that,' Edwin said, speaking in English as he usually did when the conversation revolved around emotions. Words like *sorry* and *hon* in Cantonese came out either too brittle or too syrupy.

I looked out over the railing to the avenue below, crisscrossed with lines for trams and buses and god knows what else, a mesh of wires so taut and dense that if I jumped, I'd probably bounce back up like a kid on a trampoline. Edwin's breathing beside me was slow and measured. Patient. I waited for another few seconds, watching the traffic blunder by in jolts and spurts, hoping he would explain further without prompting.

'So, what was that all about, anyway?' I finally asked, gripping the rail.

Edwin sighed. Not an impatient, distraught sigh, but a gentle, resigned exhalation. He turned toward me, slipped his fingers through my hair, smoothed the strands above my ear.

'It's hard, losing a child. A sibling. Everyone comes to terms with it in his own way. Sometimes it's easier to be angry.' He lifted my face toward his. 'Are you still hungry? Do you want to stop at a *cha chaan teng*?'

'No, I'm okay.'

I was still hungry, but the last thing I wanted was to wedge into a crowded tea house, knocking kneecaps and elbows with other diners. What I did want was to ask him what in the world the Pangs meant with the whole murderer business, but the words spinning through my mind sounded accusatory, suspicious. I looked at his eyes, tugged into right triangles with concern. This was my husband: gentle, easygoing, not a violent bone in his body. There was no way he could have anything to do with anyone's death, let alone his wife's; to ask him to explain would be to dignify an outrageous outburst by that rude loon of a father and that weird cow of a sister. The only normal Pang, the mother, was obviously on Edwin's side, so there. Completely outrageous. Not worthy of any more airtime.

'So, what's up with that dog?'

'Oh, Charming?'

'Charming?'

Edwin laughed. 'Yeah, Charming. She was Helena's. Well, ours actually. We got her when she was a puppy, but I don't think she remembers me anymore.'

'Oh.' Somehow it made me feel better that the dog didn't remember him.

'Let's go home, eh?'

As we sat in the minibus, our bodies bumping into each other as we swerved along brightly lit roads past sidewalks full of pedestrians, try as I might to push it out of my mind, all I could hear was the sound of that stupid pink dog, yapping.

\*

That night, it was my father-in-law who found me on the balcony, staring through the rails at the sleeping city below. I'd waited until Edwin was asleep before stealing out of bed, pulling on a robe, and going outside. That damn dog. Every time I closed my eyes all I could see was her stupid bow and her yapping, accusatory face. The sliding door opened with a soft whoosh and, assuming it was Edwin, I said, 'Hey, babe,' without turning around.

'*Sanpouzai?*'

I whipped around and started out of my seat.

'It's okay, you stay there,' Lou-je said, pulling over another plastic chair.

Seconds passed without either of us speaking. The night was so quiet I could hear the stutter of the crosswalk thirty-two floors below, increasing in tempo to signal safe passage to the blind. Lou-je finally spoke after the tempo had reset to a slow clip.

'So how was it with the Pangs?'

'It was okay.'

'Hmm.'

Something about his tone made me confess. 'Actually, it was awful.'

'Mm. Naai-naai and I guessed as much.'

'It's just... they don't seem to want Edwin there tomorrow.'

'What do you mean?' He hesitated before his question, as if he already knew the answer.

'They weren't very nice to him. The mother, she was okay, but the dad, the sister, even the dog seemed to hate him. They said all these horrible things—'. I stopped, wondering if I should be sharing all this with Lou-je: the piss and vinegar coming out of Mr Pang's pores, the outrageous allegation.

Lou-je let a few seconds pass before prodding. 'What things?'

A needling sensation dug into my gut, behind my belly button. It felt like a betrayal of sorts, talking to Edwin's father about the evening, but I'd already backed myself into a corner.

'They... they seem to think that Edwin has something to do with Helena's death. And I know it's ridiculous, and they all seem crazy, so I don't want to ask Edwin what they meant.'

Lou-je sighed. 'He should talk to you about it.'

'I don't want to push him.'

'Yes, but he's exposing you to them and not giving you anything to protect yourself with.'

He sighed again and settled deeper into his chair, elbows on the armrests, fingertips pressed together into a tent. It struck me how similar they were, father and son. He massaged the bridge of his nose with both index fingers, then lifted his head and began.

'You know that Edwin met Helena in high school, Form One. She was smart and pretty. Class flower. Number one in sciences.' I squirmed. Yes, the woman was gorgeous and thin and brilliant. The last thing I needed was a highlight reel.

'But then we moved to Toronto. His mother and I thought it'd be over, just puppy love, but we were wrong. Edwin proposed after he moved back to Hong Kong, fulfilling a promise he'd made when he was just a teenager. Sometimes I wonder if we were too heavy-handed when we were trying to instill a sense of duty with Edwin. I don't know. Anyway. His mother and I were not unhappy with the arrangement, though we wondered if he had closed himself off too soon.' He shook his head and added, 'Thinking back, although we had only seen her during vacations, I think we knew then that something about Helena was not quite right.'

I shifted forward, resting my elbows on my knees. It wasn't like I wanted to think ill of the dead or anything, but it was a relief to hear something other than the high-school-sweetheart fairytale I already knew.

'She was incredibly demanding of Edwin. They were impossible to separate, like sugar on beans. And as the years went by, it seemed that our son was becoming more and more weighed down. We asked him if anything was wrong, but as always, he kept things to himself. He's not much of a complainer, as you know.'

'Yeah,' I muttered. That was an understatement. After four years, I'd barely ever heard a complaint from Edwin.

Lou-je sighed. When he continued, the timbre of his voice reflected an added strain that made the skin along my hands and forearms buzz.

'Only after they were married did we find out the truth. Your Naai-naai and I moved back to Hong Kong from Toronto about a year after their wedding. We all went to Macau the second weekend we were back. It had been a while since the last time we'd seen them, and it was obvious at once that something was wrong with Helena. She had lost a lot of weight, barely ate at any meal, and was chatty one moment and completely shut down the next. Edwin was also skinny, and tired, and had these marks on the back of his hands. Naai-naai asked, and he said it was from the puppy they just adopted. We thought it was strange, but let it go. Didn't want to push him.' He let out a sharp exhalation.

'That evening, he called to say they couldn't come to dinner. We hadn't seen either of them the whole afternoon, you see, so your Naai-naai was getting worried. We walked over to their room to see how they were. Before we even reached their door, we could hear them. Or her. She was screeching at such a high pitch, at first I thought they'd brought the dog. But then I heard what she was saying. Horrible things. Hard to repeat.' He paused for a moment. 'That Edwin should kill her. That if he didn't kill her, she would kill herself. That they should both die, so that they didn't have to be in this terrible world any longer. That it wasn't her fault, and "they" were making her do it, "they" were making her miserable.'

He shrugged his shoulders, planted his hands on his thighs. I recognised then that he'd probably never told this story before; the telling itself was wearing him down to a nub.

'We knocked for close to a minute before Edwin came to the door. He was agitated. Wide-eyed. In his undershirt. That's when we saw what she had done. Up both arms all the way to his neck were a web of reddish marks, some muted like scars, and others fresh and raw; there were so many, like a tangle of wires. He didn't want us to come in but we pushed past him. The room was dark, but from what little light there was coming through the drawn shades we could see Helena in the far corner, crouched down, pointing at the opposite corner, screaming in terror. We followed where she was pointing. There was nothing there. Not even a plant or a decoration. Just an empty corner. Your Naai-naai ran out and called security. Helena suddenly got on all fours and began banging her head on the floor until Edwin wrestled her onto her back. By the time security got to the room, she was calm again. She pointed at Edwin and told the security guards that he had been beating her.

'We stood there, watching them take our son away, helpless. Since we were his parents, nothing we said could convince them that she'd struck herself instead. Days later, they put her through a psychiatric evaluation. It was some sort of schizophrenia. Edwin was let go. But he never left her. She was in and out of psychiatric wards for years; still, he never left. We barely saw him, but every time we did, he'd have some bruise or a scratch, and an excuse. Then, one night when he came home from work, he found her dead at their kitchen table. There was a bottle of wine laced with a drug. Her sister came forward with a string of emails from Helena saying that Edwin was planning to poison her, and a letter she'd written to their lawyer, saying that Edwin was after her life insurance policy. Again, the police took him in. The investigation lasted for a week or so, before the police found evidence of Helena buying the drugs herself, and let Edwin go.'

We sat for a while in silence. I could see someone in the next tower block drawing the curtains, leaving a momentary silhouette before the lights went out. Only a few flats were lit, but I wondered how many others were sitting on their balconies, invisible in the darkness, shocked out of their minds. There were too many questions. I didn't know where to begin. Why hadn't Edwin told me any of this? How could those assholes even dream of blaming my husband when it was their own deranged daughter wreaking havoc? And why were we even here for that crazy bitch? But the questions felt minor compared to the notion of Edwin suffering at the hands of a scheming psychopath. The thought of Helena raking her fingernails into him was too much. I leaned over, pressing down on the spasms in my gut. I wanted to punch her right in her pretty little face, or her sister's scrunched-up replica. I didn't even care if she was a nutcase. He stood by her and she tried to frame him for murder. Good thing we were opening the coffin tomorrow. I'd ask the bone specialist to please step aside while I bashed in the evil little skull of the deceased. And then probably end up joining her in hell. Shit.

'Get some sleep. You guys have an early start tomorrow.' Lou-je patted me on the shoulder and stood up. As he pushed open the sliding door, I called out to him softly.

'Yes?'

'Why is he going tomorrow? I mean, after all that?'

Lou-je pulled the door closed and rested his lean frame against it. He looked even thinner standing there in the moonlight.

'I think no matter what happened, Edwin still feels responsible. Despite all the things she did to him—I don't know. Sometimes I think his heart's too soft. Shoulders too wide.'

He cracked open the sliding door and said, 'Don't think too much more about it. Get some sleep.' Then he turned and slipped inside.

By dawn, I'd only slept a few hours. The more concealer I patted under my eyes, the more ghoulish I looked in my black shift. Edwin didn't look like he'd slept much either. His face had a grey pallor that matched his suit. We had to take several trains to get to the cemetery in the New Territories, but luckily not a lot of people were travelling so early on a Sunday morning. On the second-to-last train, we had the entire car to ourselves. I took his hands into mine and spoke loudly enough to be heard over the roar of the train.

'Lou-je told me what happened. I know you don't like talking about it. I just want you to know that I'm here. I am so sorry about everything you went through.'

He kept staring ahead, but his grip tightened around my fingers. From his profile, I could see tears welling in his eyes. Without a word, he put his arm around my shoulders, kissed the side of my forehead, and held me to him until it was time to change trains.

\*

When we arrived at Wo Hip Cemetery, the Pangs were nowhere in sight. After circling the outer premises, we finally found them in the waiting area of the morgue office, signing papers. Mr and Mrs Pang were appropriately outfitted in black, but the sister was in an ill-fitting red dress. The dog, once again, was a vision in pink.

'You're late,' Mr Pang said.

'I thought we were meeting out front,' Edwin replied.

'No. Inside. To sign papers.' He thrust several sheets toward Edwin. My face burned as Edwin took the papers without a word.

After the paperwork, we were all ushered into what looked like an abandoned workshop: by the entrance was a scattering of folding chairs facing two massive rectangular steel tables; on the far side of the tables were two large garbage cans, indeterminate machinery, and a metal door with a crash bar. The air was a mix of bleach and decay. On one of the tables was the coffin, mottled with dirt, weeds, and some other grey matter that I couldn't identify. The other table was covered in a white sheet marked with a faint grid of foot-long squares. For organising the bones. I handed Edwin a tissue and covered my face with another, but the momentary whiff of menthol was no match for the cloying stench. A young woman, dressed in a white coverall, mask and gloves, came in and passed around surgical masks, which everyone put on in a hurry. The dog, leashed to an exposed pipe near the wall, lay flaccid on a chair, whimpering and hiding her muzzle in one shoulder. I almost felt sorry for her. The sister sat down with a loud creak on a folding chair that was a few hairs away from collapsing and sending her to the floor. The rest of us remained standing.

At about half past nine, a tall, ruddy man with a crown of grey hair at the foot of his bald head arrived with a duffel bag. Given his profession, the bone specialist looked surprisingly robust, almost jolly. He instructed all of us to take a seat.

First, he took a long tool from the duffel bag and began wrenching open the coffin. The stench intensified tenfold. My eyes stung and salty tears ran into my mask. Mrs Pang passed around a bottle of white flower oil. After removing the lid, the bone specialist announced, 'The remains are ready.' Thank God. If the body had not sufficiently decomposed, the coffin was to be resealed and the family would have to return in six months to repeat the process. At least Helena had had the decency to rot properly. I squeezed Edwin's hand and looked over at him, wondering what he was thinking. He squeezed back, but kept his eyes on the floor.

One by one, the specialist removed the bones from the coffin, applying a white powder on his hands that made the air thick and dusty. No matter how much I tried to focus on the walls or the floor or my hands, I kept glancing at the specialist. I wondered what in the world would possess someone to take a job like this. He laid the bones into the squares on the sheet, starting with the skull and working his way down. I wanted to puke. All sorts of bad juju were probably coming off of Helena's corpse that would take a week of bathing with pomelo leaves to rid. And how long to get the stink out of our hair? Edwin's right foot was tapping repeatedly on the footrest of his chair and his palm was beginning to sweat into mine. The Pangs sat clustered together, weeping at separate frequencies and volumes. By the time the specialist laid out the femurs, the dog had pooped twice on the floor. Charming. I felt like I was stuck in one of Edwin's silent horror movies, caught in a single frame, flickering in soundless angst.

At some point, the assistant wheeled in a trolley with a brass urn that came up to the bone specialist's waist. The lip of the urn was as big around as a tyre, tapering down at the bottom to about the size of a Frisbee. The specialist started with the largest bones, laying them carefully inside, one after another. I realised that I wasn't noticing the smell as much anymore, as if my nose had decided to check out. After the last, smallest bones were placed in a white muslin bag and inserted into the urn, the specialist folded the white sheet and dumped it in the garbage receptacle behind him. Mask, gloves, and coveralls followed. The polo shirt and jeans he had on underneath seemed ridiculously out of place. He came over, hands clasped at his back.

'Mr and Mrs Pang, you may now place whatever items you have into the urn, if you wish. Do you need a bag?'

Mr Pang shook his head, unable to speak. The specialist and the assistant left the room. From her purse, Mrs Pang removed a silk drawstring bag. The sister began to wail and the dog whined in unison. Mrs Pang stepped over to where Edwin was sitting, and began to open the bag, when Mr Pang charged at her, grabbed her by the elbow and swung her around. The bag flew out of her hands in the process, scattering its contents: a handful of large gold coins, a wooden comb, a few photographs, and a complete set of pink dog booties.

'How many times do I have to tell you that he is not putting anything with my daughter?' Mr Pang's face was red and sweat was coming off of his hair as he shook his fists at his wife, who went down on her knees to retrieve the strewn items. He turned toward Edwin and yelled, 'It was you, you scum! You took her away!' For a moment, I thought he was going to deck Edwin in the face, but then he wheeled around and stomped out of the room. The sister ran after him and the dog jumped up to follow but was collared by her leash. She struggled to find her footing, slipping in her booties. Edwin bent down to help Mrs Pang up, while I remained stuck to my seat, useless.

Mrs Pang looked at Edwin, eyes full of tears, and whispered, 'I'm sorry.' Head lowered, she placed the bag into the urn and hurried out.

'I'll be right back,' Edwin said to me as he went after her, pulling off his mask to reveal a pained expression on his face.

I found myself alone with the urn and the dog. Hot tears slid down my cheeks as I unhooked my fingers from the metal rods of the chair. It was incredible. Six years dead, and Helena was still wreaking havoc, still raking her fingernails into my husband. The dog strained at her leash, yapping at the doorway. Then, having lost sight of the others, she turned around and started barking at me. Like owner, like dog. I fought the urge to kick her, or chuck her into the coffin. Then something on the floor between us caught my eye. The more I sat there, staring at her shit, smothering under the stench of Helena's rot all around us, the more pissed-off I became. I'm not sure how long I sat there, glaring, before I got up, walked over and picked up one of the hardened lumps with the tissue in my hand. It was lighter than expected, but still weighty in my palm. The dog stopped barking and cocked her head at me, this strange human holding her poop. I walked over to the urn and dropped it in. If there had ever been a time for the gates of hell to burst open and swallow me whole, that certainly would have been the moment. *That's right*, I thought, *move over already*. The dog took a step toward me. I looked down at her tiny face. She gave one short bark then pointed her nose at the other lump on the floor. I agreed. Didn't seem right to leave one behind. I retrieved the second and chucked it in after the first, tissue and all. When the assistant returned, I was back in my seat with the dog curled in my lap.

'Are they coming back?' she asked.

'I have no idea.'

She glanced alternately at the urn and the dog.

'Do you think they're done?'

'Should be.'

From the floor of the trolley, the assistant picked up the urn's heavy brass lid and twisted it carefully into place. The dog turned toward the sound of metal scraping metal. Her glossy eyes followed as the assistant wheeled the urn away. Then she looked up at me, silent. Patient, even. I stood up, unhooked her leash, and went outside to find Edwin.

He was at the front entrance consoling Mrs Pang. Mr Pang and the sister had left the grounds without her. We waited with her until a taxi came. After the taxi drove off, Edwin turned to me and asked if I was okay. I said that I was fine. He drew his shoulders back and sighed.

'That was crazy.'

'Yeah.' If he only knew. But everyone should be allowed one mystery to take to the grave.

He ran one hand through his hair and said, 'I'm so glad you're here.'

'Me, too.'

His face seemed lighter, relieved.

'Let's get the hell out of here,' I said. Then I took my husband's hand and led him down the street towards home.

# SWIMMING IN HONG KONG
## Stephanie Han

### FROGGY

She swam halfway. Instead of turning around and paddling back, she came straight forward and, with a little help from the rope, got out at the opposite end of the pool—the finish line. She didn't seem as discouraged as she did the week before. I gave a wave as I always do, and she smiled back. These things take time, but I knew it was a good sign. She's eventually going to swim a lap, that's what I told Fei Yun and Arnie. Arnie didn't believe me. Arnie's always been like that, ever since primary school. I've known him for fifty years and if he hasn't changed yet, he's not going to.

'She hasn't made it yet and she's been coming here for six months,' said Arnie.

'She's made it halfway,' I pointed out.

'I don't think she can do it. What do you want to bet?'

Arnie's always betting. A few times about ten years ago, he won money at the races. That made him feel like a big-time gambler until his wife Cherry told him that he had a choice between gambling and spending money on his grandson. That stopped it, though she lets him buy Mark Six tickets if the pot's really big. Every now and then, he likes to act as if he can bet.

'No bet,' I said.

'Why not, if you are so sure?'

'No betting. I just know. Her stroke is better. I notice her breathing has improved.'

'Froggy knows. I think she's going to make it. Whether that's in my lifetime or not is the real question,' chuckled Fei Yun.

I have had the nickname Froggy for as long as I can remember.

# Swimming in Hong Kong

I learned to swim growing up in the New Territories, and when we moved to Kowloon during my high-school days, I won a few swimming prizes. Arnie remembers. I'm also bow-legged, so it's fair to say that my nickname is due both to my former skill and my appearance.

Fei Yun, Arnie, and I come to this pool with a bunch of other old-man regulars. We were coming before we all retired and we'll be coming up until our last days. These days I come almost every day to swim outside in Victoria Park.

About six months ago this woman started coming to the pool. She's black. I overheard her tell the pool attendant that she was American. To be honest, it was the first time I've seen a black woman up close in a swimming suit. At least the first time I saw one that way who wasn't on TV. I've seen them wearing what looks like a swimming suit on those singing television programmes my grandchildren watch. Come to think of it, I don't think I've even seen a black woman swimming at the Olympics. She's slender— lean muscle, not so big. The pool attendant told me later that she's trying to train as a tri-athlete: biking, swimming, and running.

She's not a very good swimmer. The first time I saw her splashing around the pool she was gasping and flailing her limbs. Panicking: the worst thing you can do in the water. Then I realised she was grabbing onto the dividing rope and she was kicking, but nothing was wrong with her. I couldn't save her anyway if she was drowning. Not at my age. She would drown me! That's why we have the lifeguard! That's why we pay the fees! Anyway, she was hard not to notice. Gradually, her paddling began to take the shape of a crawl, and she would go about ten feet before turning around and starting again. Her eyes would widen right before she went under water, and you could tell by the way she kept trying she was going to improve. She's much better than when she first started.

I have a lot of respect for people who learn to swim as adults. My wife, Suk Mei, couldn't swim if her life depended on it. I tried to teach her when we were first married, but I wasn't patient as a young man and after a couple of lessons where I yelled at her, she didn't try again. I can't say I blame her. I taught my daughter and sons how to swim, but all of those years we spent together, my wife would watch me swim from the beach or a poolside bench. She said it didn't matter to her whether or not she could swim, but it would have been nice for her to learn. Sometimes when I am swimming in this pool I half expect her to be there when I surface. She died three years ago.

My youngest son, Man Ho, and I didn't speak for years before Suk Mei died. It was after I sent him to school in the UK and he had come back and was making a lot of money. A bigshot. He came back thinking he was better than everyone, including his own father. Bad son.

He said to me, 'If I had listened to you, I never would have made anything out of my life. What do you know?'

'I know enough to break my back to work for you and give you everything. Get out of my sight. Go back to England,' I yelled at him.

Suk Mei cried. That fancy education hadn't taught him anything. Who speaks like that to his own father? No respect. I'm the father. He didn't understand. Even now he forgets. I forgave him before Suk Mei died. Man Ho wasn't like my other kids; he always pushed the hardest, and in my heart I know that's why I loved him the most. I still do, even if I can't stand looking at how fat he's become. His body looks like a dumpling. Me, too, but I'm an old man.

I don't think the American is married. You don't get many black people in Hong Kong except around the mosques or in Central, but I'm never in Central and the only reason I was around the mosque in Tsim Sa Tsui was that my acupuncturist used to have an office there. Anyway, this is different: it is a swimming pool, not a mosque, and she is always alone.

The day she swam halfway across I passed her right before she hopped into the pool. She nodded her head and smiled, and I walked over to talk to Fei Yun. She was quiet, not that I've ever heard her speak, but her shoulders were slumped. Usually she smiles a good deal, but this time her mouth was in a straight line. Solemn. Troubled. That's why it's good to swim. I may have worries, but after I get into the pool they peel away from my body. The cool water rushes over you, a wonderful silence coats and bathes, washes everything away. In water, I feel younger than I do on land, memory flooding muscles and bones, aches disappearing. She needed to swim that day. Life is like that. There are days we all want to swim away, though the older I get, the less I have that feeling. I want to stay around as long as I can. No need to swim far; back and forth in the pool is enough. I was glad when she walked forward to the end of the pool instead of turning around. I could tell she felt better.

## RUTH

It's a start, and one must start someplace. I made it halfway, paddled then walked to the far end of the pool. Half a lap. It's getting me ready for the real thing. Usually I wade and paddle back, but not this time. Call me anything, but I'm not a quitter.

The old man in the brown swimming trunks, the one with the long eyes and sad smile, gave me a little nod. He's here whenever I am, swimming lap after lap, steady and smooth, absolutely mesmerising, the way he cuts through the water. He never tires and when he swims, he's all grace and agility, as if it's the most natural thing in the world to be submerged in the water. He does the breaststroke, hits the surface like an otter; his head bobs up for a second, he breathes, and then he's down again. When he climbs out, I'm always surprised: he really is an old man, but in the water, you wouldn't it know it.

I laugh when I think of what I must have looked like to people when I first started, or even now: a black woman desperately trying to swim to the other side, splashing all over the place, week after week, wading back as she can't get across. After years in Asia, I'm used to curious looks. Some are friendly—greeting, nodding, and watching; others never get rid of their prejudice. In Hong Kong I learned that you have to dive in because no one will wait around and ask you nicely if you're ready. Once you're in, it's a different story. You meet who you need to meet, but this is not a place for the timid.

I almost drowned when I was nine. As a child, my mother's ambition conspired with affluent day schools looking to diversify. I was good at school. My peers had homes with bathrooms larger than our apartment. One weekend I was invited with a few other girls to a friend's vacation cottage near a lake. I wanted to fit in and couldn't admit I could barely swim. The next day we were supposed to all jump off the pier and go out on a boat. To prepare, I secretly snuck down by the lake to try to practise when I thought everyone else was playing near the house. Luckily my friend's older sister pulled me out of the water. I cried with relief and shame. She tried to show me how to float, but I refused. The next day she kindly took me to town for ice cream when everyone went out on the boat. I spent the weekend playing near the cottage and reading. I'm sure the family was scared because I was never invited there again, and I didn't tell my parents either. For years, I avoided the water. It meant fitting in. I'd try, in fits and starts. Slowly. Little by little. Lessons here and there. But I never found a need to swim until six months ago. I decided it was time. The triathlon—I wanted to do it.

It's taken a long time for me to get this far swimming—six months to hit the middle, but I'll make it across. I learned that from running, the challenge of pushing through; it's that easy and that hard. I finally felt ready to swim. As masochistic as it sounds, I'm a great believer in doing whatever it is you find difficult. This is both positive, when it comes to work, and dare I say, negative when it comes to relationships: there are people who are difficult for a reason—and there is no need to hang around!

There are days when all I want to do is to jump in the water and swim all the way to India, from work and everything else in my life. I say I'm good at leaving and moving, though I'm no longer sure if it's true. As I grow older, I find myself growing less comfortable with picking up and moving, which is disturbing because I am not certain where it is that I want to be. But I don't think it's here. People back home me ask why I'm still in Hong Kong. It's a perfectly valid question and one I periodically ask myself, but I've been an expatriate for many years and have lived in many places — London, Sydney, Rome, Tokyo. I have no plans to go stateside, and I remain unconvinced about the benefits of American life. Or maybe it's that there's nothing for me to return to, no one to return for.

Earlier that day before swimming, my boss refused to give me Lunar New Year's *lai see*. He's the definition of the glory-seeking,

Ivy League-educated elitist. Having an Ivy League education myself, I feel perfectly entitled to call him that. If I had been in any other office in Hong Kong, I would have received a slim New Year's red envelope with crisp bills from the bank, as not only have I been an employee at this architecture firm for four years, but I'm single. He's Chinese, and spent twelve years in the US, but illustrious institutions can breed a reprehensible lot. He, unfortunately, has failed to distinguish himself from the pack. He's the typical self-aggrandising male hell-bent on making others miserable. Tyrants of his ilk have remarkable geographic mobility—they're everywhere. It's actually astounding how people like him feel the need to spread their horrid personalities across the continents.

My firm is doing the huge project on the waterfront, the complex of restaurants, offices and apartments that are part of Hong Kong's effort to revitalise the tourist industry post-Handover. We've managed to convince (dare I utter the words *bribery* or *coercion*?) the regulatory bodies that by further filling in the harbour and creating more pollution than ever before, and erecting yet another concrete tower, we will be helping to make Hong Kong a world-class city that everyone will once again want to visit. I'm cynical—perhaps I've been in this profession too long—but then again, what architect isn't?

Our office is white, glass, and steel. Neat employee lockers in perfect slate grey. Small cubicles of clear soundproof boxes, an office of the present, future, and past. I confess to admiring the sleek lines and precision, the fact that everything is perfectly accounted for, measured and thought out—down to the height of an unsharpened pencil, so that when you place the pencil in your exquisite company-issued pencil holder, the shelf space will barely skim its pink eraser. The office lighting in meeting rooms magically erases fine lines and succeeds in making everyone's skin appear smooth and supple. Every detail is designed to improve employee productivity and put clients at ease. The talent it took to create this and other structures is inarguably stupendous. Yet talent doesn't have anything to do with being a tolerable human being, which he, my boss, the creator of this space, is most certainly not.

He stood by the door to my office and then announced in a loud booming voice: 'You're too old for *lai see*. It's for single people who aren't married. You're so old, you're supposed to be giving *lai see* away and already married.' He chuckled.

Too old. He knows I'm forty-one. My colleague Janice heard that, and so did Charlie. They thought it was nasty, if not cruel, of him to say that. I'm the only Westerner in the office, so he probably thought he could get away with it.

'Too old. It's not about that. You're supposed to say, "Happy New Year, Ruth, wishing you all the best and I hope you get yourself a good husband this year and have much happiness." Age has nothing to do with New Year's etiquette.' I turned around and sat behind my desk and watched him slink away towards the water cooler.

He didn't respond. It did shut him up. Like all Ivy Leaguers, he shudders to think he's behaved in a gauche manner. The nature of his personality is such that to ignore him invites further insults. He's a few years older than I am and always comments on my hair, my clothes, something personal. It's never a compliment, more of an observation, as in 'you changed your hair' or 'you're wearing red, you never wear red' or 'you lost weight'. Or he'll insult me and publicly state that my Cantonese is lousy after living here for ten years. Or bring up my marital status. (He doesn't know about my divorce, but that's my business.) It's subtle, but Janice notices.

'He likes you. You know. *Likes* you. I think he finds you attractive,' she said delicately.

'Oh, for god's sake. Please do not even say those words.'

'Why?' she giggled.

'Why? He's married with three children, and he is absolutely the last person I'd want to imagine in that kind of scenario.' I wasn't surprised when she said it, but what a Freudian nightmare—another reason to prefer Jung. The paralysis would be too intense if one actually followed Freud's theories to their conclusion.

'That's true. He's not someone anyone would like. But he likes you. That's why he's so mean.'

'He likes me so much that he cuts my salary twenty percent, makes me work on Sundays, and calls me at all hours of the night and day to tell me to come into the office. He says I'm too old to get married. If that's his idea of affection, I pity the woman he loves! Last week, he said he thought I looked like I'd gained weight. The man is a true beast.'

'You know when children are on the playground and one child likes another, maybe he hits her to show affection? It's like that. Very immature,' she said.

'That's right. Nursery behaviour. That's ridiculous. I'm not interested. Why would I find him the least bit interesting?'

'Because he's rich and is your boss?'

'He's married, has no personality, and drives his employees into the ground. And let's face it, he obviously hasn't hit the gym in the last ten years. The only reason I take this crap from him is that there aren't any other jobs. I'm single, but I'm not desperate. There may not be a lot of jobs out there, but there are definitely other men.'

I sounded funny, but I was fuming. Janice laughed. Charlie heard the last part and raised his eyebrows.

I didn't add, but it was clearly understood, that should a black-woman-and-Chinese-man pairing occur, it certainly would not be us. I am loath to ponder that twisted brain of his, which is probably filled with adolescent jungle-bunny *National Geographic* fetishes I don't want to explore. The combination doesn't happen much anyway. It does in Jamaica: my father's sister married a Chinese man, but it's a rare occurrence outside of that world. I find Chinese men attractive and I'm no fool. I've been in situations where they fancied me, not just my boss, but the pairing eludes.

Make that overall in Hong Kong. Dating isn't easy here, but it's not as if I'm looking only to date a black man, and I never dated much anyway. I had a brief marriage to a white British journalist whose family thought me exotic. I believe that my Josephine Baker hairdo (then) and Italian language skills might have fuelled the perception. My family just wanted him out. They were incredibly racist, but there were other reasons the marriage failed—specifically, *a* reason. She's got him now.

I focus on my work. I run. I'm learning to swim. When we buried my father in Jamaica, I looked out onto the blue and imagined him swimming there years ago, stopping at the well to get water on the way back home to the weathered wooden shack. That old dusty road, the sections of grass and black rocks and sand. The tree he described as being so tall, the tallest tree he'd ever seen, and the ripe guava you want to grab from the branch. He would tell us stories about his life, his language becoming lyrical as the stories unfolded, aching with longing for the village he left. He never went back after he came to the US—he left a beautiful land, blue water, desperate hot sun, and sand that burned your eyes with its whiteness for the American dream.

What he left behind was hard to square with the adult I knew, the man who navigated cold grey sidewalks and tall buildings. Sometimes I try to imagine him. Not as my father, but as someone I didn't know, a boy with everything before him, oceans away from his future. He always said he was a good swimmer, but the way he struggled and where we lived, there was never time for him to show me.

## FROGGY

She stopped at the halfway point.

The last three times I've seen her, that's what has happened. She's hit a plateau.

Fei Yun shook his head, 'Not in my lifetime.'

'Be quiet,' I said loudly.

Fei Yun shrugged. 'She's getting discouraged. She didn't get to the end.'

You can always count on Fei Yun to be gloomy. He had some hard times as a kid. During the war, his parents and sisters died. He says the war taught him to prepare for the worst. And later, after nearly his whole family died, during those bad years in China, he swam to Hong Kong. Tolo Harbour. Took guts.

'A piece of wood can save your life,' is all he usually says about it, other than that the cousin he left with drowned. Fei Yun's done well. He's got an import-export business. Just don't talk to him about the old days in China.

'We had to take our pots and pans. Everything. Melt it all down. You know what you get when you throw a pot on the fire?'

'No,' we all say. We do this every time.

'A pot that won't melt,' he says. That's when he decided to leave. Just him and his cousin.

Arnie was the one who sounded hopeful: 'I think she'll make it. She needs some technique advice.'

'Her breathing is slowing her down. She comes up too soon for air. She needs to turn her head all the way to the side,' I said. The black woman needed some swimming lessons. That's what Fei Yun and Arnie were trying to say.

'I think it's her kick,' said Arnie.

'It's both,' I said. 'The crawl is very difficult. People are fooled. Took me a long time. Did you see her on TV?'

'For what? Singing?' asked Fei Yun.

'Now why would she be singing? What makes you think she can sing?' I said. Why would a famous singer be swimming three times a week in a public pool in Victoria Park? Sometimes Fei Yun is so thick. 'No, she was running in the marathon.'

'Marathon, eh? Didn't see it,' said Fei Yun.

'Did she win?' asked Arnie. I knew he was thinking he should have placed a bet.

'No, she was running in it. She runs very fast,' I lied. She was actually walking on TV. She looked tired. What do I care?

'Then why can't she swim?' asked Arnie.

'What does swimming have to do with running, you stupid idiot!' At this point I had to walk away. After fifty years, talk like this can really get on your nerves.

When the black woman hoisted herself up out of the pool, I waved to her. She studied me as I showed her how the elbow pulls back in tandem with the head as it turns to the side, like a clock, all the parts, the teeth, like cogs moving forward in synchrony. She tried it once at the side of the pool by the ladder while I watched and corrected her. Then she said thank you, got in, and prepared to do a lap.

At first when she happened to pass me she wouldn't say anything, but I guess she noticed that we were always there. We say hi or hello. I can understand some English, but I'm not really comfortable saying much more than that. She speaks some Cantonese: Good morning. Hello. Bye-bye.

We all stood and watched her. I told Arnie and Fei Yun they

really should go away, not make such a big deal about it, but of course they went about three steps and kept looking over their shoulders watching to see if she could do it, all the while pretending to towel off.

She almost got it. She made it about two-thirds of the way across. Fast learner. She didn't turn her head quite like she should, but her stroke was much better. She grinned and paddled to the end of the pool, using the divider ropes to get to the end. She did it two more times, not going all the way, maybe half.

I thought to myself that there must not have been anyone to teach her. Maybe no one in her family knows how to swim. What do they think of her living in Hong Kong? I remember when Man Ho was in England. I was always worrying, though never out loud because Suk Mei was always going on about it, so someone had to pretend that he was fine so far away. That's a man's job.

What's she doing here? Her parents must worry. There could be a number of reasons why she didn't learn to swim as a child. Did anyone know she was swimming now?

My sons were fine swimmers. The youngest, Man Ho, could swim the butterfly. Perfect kicking, just like a dolphin. You'd never know it looking at him; these days he's such a fat bastard. Rich, but fat. Last week at the restaurant, I told him he ate too much.

'Slow down. Moderation,' I said to him.

'I'm not eating much,' he said defensively.

'You eat too much. You won't live long.' It's about the only thing I can tell him these days.

'I'm living well. Those who live well, live long,' he said licking the tips of his chopsticks. For a moment when he looked at me, I saw him as a baby, nearly bald, with an open round face, chubby arms and fists waving in the air. He never listens. I didn't say anything.

One vacation I put him in a tiny inner tube and pulled him around a pool, letting it glide along the water as the waves rippled out, skimming the surface. I used to skip stones. I could skip them maybe seven or eight times. My kids couldn't do that growing up in the city. We took them to the parks on the weekend, but it's not the same.

Out in the New Territories I always had plenty of places to run around and swim. Me and Arnie. I swam in water that was real, not chlorinated. Swimming outside, you can see the trees. There was the walk home on the path where you had to duck your head under the branch in the middle of the path and you were always afraid it was going to fall on you.

Now I'm a city swimmer. At night during the summer is best. Look up at the purple black sky, the neon lights of the building. When the moon is up, right over the buildings, that's something. That neon sign just dances on the water.

Funny the details you remember about your child growing up, about yourself, growing up.


## RUTH

Finished the race. I was pleased to have accomplished that. People go on about their times, but for me, it's just about finishing. I met the winner, Femi, after the race when all the participants were milling around and congratulating each other.

'You did great,' Femi said.

'Thanks. So did you. Congratulations.'

'Thank you. Have you been training a long time?' he asked.

'Several months, at least for this race. What about you?'

'My whole life.'

'Good thing you won. Wouldn't want you to have wasted your life. Do you race often?' I don't know why I said that or asked him that dumb question. It was clear he was a professional, but I have a tendency to get nervous and behave strangely in front of men I'm attracted to.

Femi pointed to his shoes: 'My sponsor. I train in France.'

He's a professional athlete from Kenya. Usually, I don't go for African guys; they can be a bit macho for me, but he was different. I'm keeping my options open. He's off for another series of races in Europe where he's sponsored.

After the race a bunch of us went out to eat, and we sat next to each other. He's left-handed and I'm right-handed, so we kept touching elbows, which was nice, really. He kept apologising and I kept telling him that it wasn't an issue and then, somewhere towards the end of the evening, our elbows were touching, and neither of us was moving away.

'I'd like to see you again,' he said.

'Oh.' I felt shy. I looked at his left earlobe.

'Can I come to visit you? I have a holiday coming up.'

What could I say? 'Sure,' I said, smiling. I couldn't stop. I'm dreadfully obvious when I fancy someone.

'Do you have vacation time?'

I nodded and got really chatty. Next thing I knew, I was blabbing about my vacation time, running, holidays, travelling, my family.

They televised the marathon; my big embarrassing moment as the camera was on me while I was walking instead of running. People saw, including my boss.

'I saw you on television. You were wearing too many clothes. I mean, it was hot out,' my boss said.

'That's what you wear for a marathon,' I answered. I thought Janice was going to have a heart attack. Later I said to her, 'He expected me to wear a short running top and shorts.'

'What were you wearing?'

'Leggings and a T-shirt. I had my running bra on underneath. It's not a fashion parade. I know what he wants and I'm not here for that. What a loser.'

Later my boss tried to explain himself and went off on this tangent about sponsorship advertisements and how leggings absorb sweat—to cover up what, as Janice said, was a completely inappropriate statement. Everyone on my team heard his comments. Charlie's ears burned red and Janice almost spilled her coffee.

'He says too much,' said Charlie before turning back to his computer.

If Charlie is adding his part, it has to be bad, as he's just not the sort to jump in, so I know I'm not imagining this situation with my boss. Janice began to call our boss a pervert whenever he was out of sight. The Pervert this, the Pervert that, the Pervert wants so-and-so. I told her she'd better stop or she'd have the entire office calling him that. She's half my size and twice as loud.

After my boss made his huge blunder, he told me I had to do a site inspection on Sunday. When I asked, due to all of my overtime these past months, if and when I was going to get my salary reinstated, which would effectively be a raise, he had the nerve to laugh.

'Why should you get a raise?'

'Because I'm the only damn person who can do this job in the entire company.' I was calm when I said it, but we were past the pretence of superficial politeness. We'd known each other for four years.

'The economy. No can do, Ruth You have to give me some reasons. Put it together in a package I can present,' he said reluctantly. Hong Kong has tanked, it's true. Everyone's heading to Shanghai. I threw him a look. He knew what I said was true and he was worried. He has to ask the higher-ups, but what do they care?

I need this job now. I have bills to pay. But I've got to look around for something else.

The old man with the brown trunks helped me with my breathing, and as a result I made it two-thirds of the way across. Funny, those old guys. I quite like them. I went early in the morning and he was there with his friends. He gestured to have me try the crawl by the side of the pool, and he told me not to bend my legs so much when I kick, to pull my head to the side.

I tried to do what he said, but didn't seem to get anywhere. I shook my head and said I was tired, told him I would try again, and he said I need to try to move with it, and not fight it so hard.

My broken Cantonese and his broken English and lots of pantomime, but I got it. When I went back in, my stroke improved. When I surfaced, the old man smiled and told me to go home and rest. I told him I had to go to work, and he told me to think about swimming at the office. If I did this, he joked, I may not do so well at work, but my swimming would get better. Let the rhythm and feeling dive into your bones, let the water guide you—I knew that was what he tried to convey through his gestures. I can do it when I run, but when I swim I panic and then have to reason with myself: *there's no need to be afraid*. It's a constant struggle.

I remember floating in college, my first boyfriend Dan firmly holding my back as I kept insisting that I sank, that I was not meant to swim. He encouraged me slowly, holding me up, first with both hands, then one, then a few fingers, lightly touching my back, so I could barely feel him. Knowing he was there gave me confidence. Then one day, it happened, he let go and I was floating. The fact that I swim at all was due to him. We broke up as all people do in college, over some silly jealousy or misunderstanding. At forty-one, the reasons you have at twenty-one for ending a relationship seem irrelevant. Expectations change.

I don't rely on anyone. I'm very independent, though I'm not sure if it's by choice. Last time I was stateside, I heard Dan was divorced with two kids. I thought about calling him, but never did. I was too busy coping with my father's death, my mother's mourning, my collapsed marriage.

I remember stepping off the plane for my father's funeral, touching ground in the US for exactly six hours before meeting up with eighteen family members, none of whom had ever flown before and were extremely nervous about getting on a plane to Jamaica. All of us going back to bury my father. *Don't you bury me in the US*, he said. *I lived here sixty years, but home is Jamaica. That is where my bones will rest.*

The funeral was the last time I cried over someone. I can't seem to squeeze the salt from my eyes anymore.

**FROGGY**

After one good lesson, she improved, but there must be something going on. If possible, she's gotten worse in the last week. She's not getting any farther, splashing around, not concentrating. If I knew English I might have yelled at her, told her to keep her legs straight and not to flop around so much. Breathe evenly. Nothing worse than to watch someone with potential mess up. She's trying too hard. It happens.

When Man Ho was first learning, he would get it really fast. Then for several weeks he seemed to get worse. Couldn't figure it out. He was small, maybe seven years-old—a little boy.

'What's wrong with you. You forgot everything we did just a week ago? How come you forgot?'

'I can't remember,' he said tearfully.

'It's because you're thinking too much. What are you thinking about?'

'Nothing,' he said, shaking his head.

'You have to be thinking about something. Don't think so much when you're swimming. Then your body can remember.'

That day he didn't swim well. But then a week later, he was swimming better than ever. I was so proud of him. I couldn't help it. I taught him. He's my son.

## RUTH

I thought my boss was going to lose it.

'You can't quit,' he said loudly.

'Of course I can quit. And I am quitting. One month's notice, as required.'

'I was going to talk about the raise,' he said quietly. He looked upset.

'You mean reinstating my salary, or a raise on top of that?'

'A raise.'

'I'll think about it,' I said, enjoying every second of his anxiety.

'You're a good worker, important to the company,' he said. As if I'm supposed to be a happy worker? I am not a happy communist worker, or even a happy capitalist worker. We done left the plantation. Christ. But, I admit, I am thinking about it, in a vague distant way you think about a job that you no longer want.

## FROGGY

She did it! I knew she would. She got in the pool as usual and started swimming, even kicks, a powerful pull, but without using too much energy, she turned her head the right amount to get some air.

When she hit the halfway mark, even Arnie and Fei Yun stopped jabbering. Arnie and Cherry might go on a gambling cruise, so that's all he's been talking about. The American made them stop talking. Her swimming was confident.

'Hey Froggy, I think she's going to make it! Want to bet?' joked Arnie.

'No, I don't want to bet you fool. I've been telling you she's going to make it from the beginning,' I said.

'Her technique is better. Slightly,' said Fei Yun.

When she touched the end of the pool we all started clapping and cheering. Congratulations! Well done!

She started crying.

I thought Fei Yun was going to start bawling himself. Even Arnie shut up about the cruise for a moment and handed her a towel. Some of the other guys who've been watching clapped too and came over to offer her congratulations.

I was so happy. I said, 'Congratulations!' about six times. What else is there to say? This is an Olympic-length pool. Not everyone can make it across, get to the other side.

Next thing she has to learn is a flip turn. It's fine for old guys like me or Fei Yun to touch the side, though even I do some flip turns now and then. But Ruth's young enough to do a proper turn when she finishes a length. That's the best way!

I should ask Man Ho to come swim with me. We don't see each other much and I bet he hasn't swum in years. He golfs. What kind of exercise is that? Riding around in a cart, hitting a little ball, and then eating and drinking afterwards until you have to undo your belt. Bad exercise I tell you, from the looks of him. Whenever I see him, he's gained more weight. It'd be a shame if he never swam again. He was a fine swimmer.

## RUTH

I applied for a visa and bought my ticket to India. I told Janice to come over to my flat as I was getting rid of my possessions.

'Here. My very favourite ultra-sexy top. Very small on me, but on you, it'll be bigger. It's sexy, don't you think?' I held up the lacy purple top and Janice took it and put it in the corner with other treasured castoffs I had given her: a few Balinese bowls, knick-knacks from Thailand, baskets, blank photo albums.

'No, I can't take that,' Janice said when I gave her a necklace of glass beads.

'Why?'

'You told me a long time ago your husband gave that to you. It's sentimental. You have to keep that.'

'Janice, I divorced him.'

'Maybe you had some good memories.'

'Some. Very few. And I can remember them fine without this. Besides, it goes with the purple top.'

'Did he give you the purple shirt?' she asked with surprise.

'No. But it goes. He liked me wearing purple. It's really not my colour. I feel like a big grape when I wear it. If you don't take it, I'll toss it. I'm trying to start over, make a new beginning.'

'Okay, okay. Ruth,' she said hesitantly. 'I wish you good luck. You think you'll come back to Hong Kong?'

I didn't know how to answer her. I will never live here again. She looked at me hopefully. 'I'll be back to visit. Hong Kong is inside of me,' I said patting my chest. 'It's there and has me— inside. I'll come back.'

'Hong Kong will miss you,' she said. We hugged goodbye, and I waved as she walked out to the minibus. She was happy for me, but I felt sad. Truthfully, it will be a long time, if ever, before we see each other again.

I'm good at moving and leaving. In a few months Hong Kong will seem like a long time ago. I remember the feeling of starting over and having the world seem new, waiting to be opened. I have a few contacts, but I haven't made any plans and don't know if I'll stay there long enough to get a job. I'll be meeting Femi in Goa after his race in Thailand. These fences and goals you have, ticking them off as the years pass, you begin to wonder why the rush, what is it all for? My father's favourite topic for discussion the last ten years of his life was not just his own non-existent pension plan, but mine, and he undoubtedly would be turning in his grave right now. *What's your plan? Where are you going?* Fair enough. Good questions.

I swam my lap. The old men clapped and cheered, and I started to cry. I was glad I made it across the water. It's a very long swimming pool.

## FROGGY

When Man Ho showed up at the pool, I was surprised. I told him I'd be there in the morning, but I didn't really expect him to show up, despite the invitation. I was pleased, but tried not to let on.

'Should we swim a lap?' he asked me.

'Go right ahead. Think you remember?'

'My body remembers.'

When Man Ho jumped in, I thought he'd empty the pool! This is what happens when you try to swim when you're that big. I hope he keeps exercising. I worry about him, and I'm too old for that. He's supposed to be worrying about me!

I swam a few laps, and he was there, right at my tail. This means I'm either swimming fast for an old man or he's too fat to keep up. Or maybe he's just letting me lead the way for once in his life.

'Do you want to race?' I asked him when I got to the end of the pool.

'I never race when I know I'll be beaten,' he said, smiling.

My son is an excellent swimmer.

# THE TROUBLED BOYHOOD OF BALDWIN WONG
Peter J. Phillips

## I. Inauspicious Beginnings

There are generations in all great bloodlines to whom genetics are not kind. For the Wongs, the boy's name was Baldwin, and he was born in the autumn of 1976.

That Baldwin Wong came from money was obvious, if only from the aristocratic names of his father and uncles: Crawford, Archibald, and Horatio. Together, the brothers enjoyed membership privileges at no fewer than seven Hong Kong clubs. Baldwin's mother, Anita, had exquisite cheekbones and a figure custom-made for a cheongsam. She had competed with distinction in the 1972 Miss Hong Kong pageant, before marrying Crawford at age twenty-three. Into her fifties, she possessed flawless, buttery skin, which was providential for Crawford, as his principal business was skin creams. On big race days at Sha Tin, he would parade her around the owner's box as proof that his Forever Jeune line worked miracles. In truth, Anita only ever used La Mer.

After the pageant, TVB occasionally hired Anita for non-speaking roles in its period dramas. She once played the concubine of a Tang Dynasty emperor. All this stopped when she fell pregnant with Baldwin. What didn't stop was Anita's love affair with cigarettes, and she continued to smoke two packs of Pall Mall Gold ('puff for puff, milder than ever') each day of Baldwin's gestation. The paediatrician Lionel Tsang told colleagues that he suspected this was the cause of the mild cranial deformity Baldwin was born with.

The boy had an abnormally shaped skull: his eyes were too widely set, his forehead jutted outwards. After six months, Dr

Tsang successfully operated, although the surgery left a zigzagging scar across the top of Baldwin's head. How deep his emotional scars zigzagged, we shall see later. For nearly a year, Baldwin had to wear a little blue helmet while his remoulded skull hardened. Unsurprisingly, only a few photographs of him from this period survive.

Despite all this, Crawford and Anita were relieved to have produced a male heir, something Crawford's brothers had failed to do. It meant that decisions regarding more progeny could be deferred until later. When later came, however, they found themselves busy with other things. Crawford, for example, opened two factories in Shenzhen when the city was declared a Special Economic Zone in 1980. Each quarter, he travelled across the border, staying fortnights at a time as the business grew. Fearful he would take a mainland mistress, Anita heeded Olivia Newton-John's 1981 call to get physical, and began aerobics. She decided that more children would only blight her figure, and secretly went on the pill.

## II. Playground Beltings

Because Anita had been raised a Catholic, she was adamant that Baldwin be educated by an order of brothers. They chose the Jesuits of Saint Augustine's, whose brochures promised *a liberal education based on Christian principles*. There was nothing Christian about the treatment served up to Baldwin. From day one of primary school, he was taunted about his misshapen head. In 1983, when Stephen Spielberg's *E.T.* was released in Hong Kong, some of the boys took to calling him just that. Once, in the change rooms after P.E., a mob of them pinned Baldwin down on a slatted bench. They emitted high-pitched yelps as Ronald So poured warm urine from a milk bottle over Baldwin's silky white shorts. 'E.T. pee pee,' they sang.

That night, they continued to pursue Baldwin in his dreams, chasing him down an endless corridor of lockers. At first it was only Ronald and a few others, but the further Baldwin ran, the more tormentors emerged from the lockers. Soon there were dozens of manic schoolboys closing in. Awake, Baldwin ran to Anita's bedroom, where he found his mother propped up by pillows, reading one of her Agatha Christies, smoking. He threw himself onto Crawford's vacant side of the bed, sobbing.

'You know you can't sleep with Mummy,' she eventually said, bookmarking her Christie.

'Not even tonight?' Baldwin said.

Anita ran her fingers along Baldwin's hairline, feeling the ridge of his scar. 'Your father wouldn't like it,' she said.

'He doesn't have to know. It can be our secret.'

'I'll come and lie with you till you sleep.'

As a teenager, Baldwin's appearance gradually improved, as Dr Tsang had predicted. By fifteen, he was taller than his father, and due to an asthma-combating regimen of swimming, he had developed broad, athletic shoulders. Baldwin loved being in the pool. With his swim cap and goggles on, there was nothing the other boys could tease him about. He churned through the water like a cigar boat, breaking five freestyle records during his time at Saint Augustine's.

At sixteen, Baldwin acquired jowls that made his forehead seem less pronounced, his face less out of proportion. Had he unattractive parents, he might have passed as tolerable. Problem was, Anita was as beautiful now as she was in her Miss Hong Kong sash twenty years ago, while Crawford carried off the distinguished silver-fox look of a Patek Philippe ad.

On days when they attended luncheons at the yacht/cricket/racquet club, Anita always noticed the commiserative expressions of the other mothers. 'Why Anita,' they would say, 'your boy has grown so big.' She knew what they were thinking: *Why Anita, under no circumstances shall you ever suggest an alliance between my Evelyn and THAT.*

Baldwin understood this too, and developed the habit of staring at his shoes during polite conversation. This displeased Crawford. 'Baldwin,' he would say, 'a good businessman always looks people in the eye.'

Anita was unfazed by these setbacks. She realised that all mothers of teenage daughters believe their little angels are destined to marry handsome princes. Only when the daughters hit their twenties do the mothers regain sense and urgency.

'You wait,' she assured Baldwin. 'Five years from now, you'll be the most eligible young man in this club.'

'You think so?' said Baldwin, wanting to believe.

'Think so? I *know* so.'

It was entirely a matter of money, and with Crawford about to announce Forever Jeune's expansion into Taiwan, the Wongs had more than most. Soon, Anita thought, they would be rich enough for her to not only match Baldwin with anyone in the yacht/cricket/racquet club she wanted—she could marry off the family dog too if she liked!

In his final year of high school, Baldwin discovered reading. With his classmates out wielding their fake IDs in Lan Kwai Fong, he stayed home in Kowloon Tong and stared down Tolstoy. On a dare from his English teacher Brother Davies, he conquered *War and Peace* over the summer of 1994.

'I read Tolstoy,' said Crawford, on a rare evening he was home. '*Anna Karenina*. Sixth Form.'

'What did you think?' asked Baldwin, looking up from his book for the first time in hours. He had been neck-deep in the Napoleonic Wars since lunch.

'Good story,' said Crawford, 'although terribly long. How are your other subjects going?'

'You're worried I'm spending too much time reading.'

It was true: Crawford couldn't compute how his son's love of literature would help with business. He had visions of his factories in flames, as Baldwin, Nero-like, sat idly with his head in a book. 'Not worried,' he said. 'Curious.'

'I'm topping Maths and Chemistry, but alas,' Baldwin said, theatrically dropping his head to his hands, 'I'm only coming second in Economics.'

'Ronald So?'

'Not since Year Eight, Pa. Hiren Patel.'

'Indian?'

'Does he sound Chinese?'

At the Saint Augustine's valedictory assembly, Baldwin was named Runner-up to Dux and winner of the Cardinal's Prize for Best All-Rounder. After inauspicious beginnings, he had truly excelled at high school. Champion swimmer. Scholar. Survivor. He would have his pick of universities.

'Surely you will choose Cambridge,' said Anita, as they dined after the ceremony. 'The Wongs have attended Cambridge since your grandfather.'

'Ma, you know I'm going to Stanford,' Baldwin said. He had already received two provisional acceptance letters, but like the faint varicose veins on her legs, Anita wanted them not to be real.

'Stanford's the right choice,' Crawford said. 'It's ranked top ten in the world, and there are lots of exciting things happening in California.'

'Like what?' Anita said.

'Um, like computers,' said Baldwin. His condescending tone met with one of Anita's well-rehearsed glares. 'All the big players are there.'

'Big players,' said Anita with a humph. 'What about tradition?'

## III. Campus Doldrums

'No falling in love with American girls,' said Anita in the noisy, smoke-filled Aviators' Bar at Kai Tak airport. Baldwin would board for SFO in an hour.

'As if,' Baldwin said, embarrassed.

'I'm serious,' Anita said. 'You're the last male in the Wong bloodline. We need to find you a nice Chinese girl *here*.'

'Ma, you're talking like a racist.'

'Not racist. I care about the family name. Wish you cared too.'

'What if the American girl was Chinese?'

'What do you mean?'

'You do realise, Ma, that Stanford has one of the highest Asian-American student populations.'

'It's true,' Crawford said, double-checking the bill before signing. 'My friend Wilfred Chen says the same thing.'

'Not the same,' said Anita. 'What do you want a college girl for anyway? I didn't go to college, and look how happy I make Daddy.' She looked to Crawford for affirmation, but he was synchronising his watch to the digital clock on the wall.

'You two met in the seventies, Ma. We've had two or three waves of feminism since then, depending on who you read.'

'You and your theories. Remember, you're going to America to study, not waste your time with girls.'

'I know, Ma. Don't worry.'

Anita need not have. From the moment Baldwin arrived on campus, there was never any possibility of him having a Californian tryst. Not because he shared his mother's view that the Wong bloodline must not be contaminated with non-Hong Kong genes, but because Baldwin had zero confidence. And by zero confidence, we don't mean shy and awkward, we mean *absolute* zero, the null point of the confidence scale.

Witness a Palo Alto house party he attended a month into his freshman year. The theme was 'IN-Continental' (subheading: 'Party till you piss yourself!') and around the backyard were no fewer than seven drink stations. Each was named after one of the world's main continuous land masses. Baldwin spent most of his night near Antarctica, where a guy in a ski jacket and balaclava served frozen daiquiris in between smoking spliffs and shooting people with a water pistol. Half an hour before the cops shut down the party, Baldwin found himself conversing with a thickset sophomore from Albuquerque.

'So where you from?' she said.

Baldwin backed away at the smell of her breath, a repulsive mixture of cigarettes, chili dog, and beer. 'Hong Kong,' he said.

'Rock on,' she said. 'My little brother's a massive Bruce Lee fan.'

'Did you know he was born not far from here? San Francisco Chinatown, 1940.'

'What are you, some kind of kung-fu nerd?'

'Bruce Lee's a compulsory subject in all Hong Kong schools. Eighth and ninth grade.'

'Really?' said the sophomore, unsure whether Baldwin was joking. She grabbed a handful of his butt and squeezed, then pressed her chest into his.

'Hey,' she said, her fumes more toxic than ever. Baldwin noticed a butterfly transfer on her cleavage, half washed away by the night's spillage. 'This year I want to fuck someone from every continent. Want to be China?'

Before Baldwin had time to process her question, the girl was vomiting into a flowerpot. He held her greasy locks with one hand, gently stroked her back with his other. He had observed

Crawford do this for Anita after Uncle Horatio's sixtieth. He didn't know it then, but this episode with Laurie from Albuquerque would be the closest he came to losing his virginity at Stanford.

He became convinced that his childhood antagonists from Saint Augustine's were right: he really was from outer space, light years away from any earthly woman desiring him. By his senior year, he'd taken to spending entire weekends locked in his dorm room. He masturbated with the compulsion of a smoker, losing himself in grainy twenty-second clips of women with silicone breasts riding the sybian. Sometimes the whole experience was ruined when, mid-act, he caught sight of his forehead in the reflective glass of the monitor. He would let go of his cock and lean into the mesh back of his chair. He would remember having warm piss poured on him by Ronald So in primary school. He would gaze at the woman on the screen with a dildo still inside her, knowing that he would never taste the flesh of someone like her, never be free of his past.

Sometimes Anita would call during these moments, and without pulling up his tracksuit pants, Baldwin would sit there and listen to her jabber on about another of her friends' children's nuptials.

'Remember Veronica Mui?' she would ask. 'Just been to her daughter's wedding in Repulse Bay. Beautiful reception. Do you know the worst thing?'

'You missed having your dashing son to accompany you.'

'Don't be facetious, Baldwin.' *Facetious*: no doubt a *Reader's Digest* Word of the Month. 'Nearly all my friends,' she continued, 'see their children married already. They keep asking, "Anita, when's your big day?" Do you know how hard that is?'

'But Ma, you told me not to waste time on girls until after college. Remember?'

She did. And this reminder calmed her, temporarily. It was Baldwin who wasn't convinced. What if he *couldn't* find someone after college? What if all the eligible young women of Hong Kong really were vanishing off the market, like Anita made it seem?

In his final semester, Baldwin tired of Internet porn and developed a sudden passion for tennis. As with swimming in high school, sport became his escape from the loneliness that was life as Baldwin Wong. He was a natural and rapidly developed a reputation for possessing one of the best two-handed backhands on campus.

Crawford was thrilled when he heard the news. 'Son,' he said over the phone, 'good racquet skills will take you far in Hong Kong. You know I used to play?'

'For the Jockey Club.'

'Before you were born. I'm going to nominate you for membership at the Colonial Club though. They have the best courts, but for decades one of the worst teams.'

'But Pa, I'm really still a beginner.'

'That's what not what your mother says. Look, I know the pro at the Olympic Club. Frank DiMarco, used to coach in Hong Kong. You're going to have lessons with him.'

Frank was a rake-thin Italian immigrant in his forties, ironically nicknamed Chubby. He had golden, leathery skin and a wardrobe comprised exclusively of primary-colour Lacoste shirts. 'I used to be a contender,' he told Baldwin when he met him. This meant he played a couple of satellite tournaments in the eighties, before finding a home in the country clubs of the Hamptons, then Hong Kong, now San Francisco.

'Just caress it,' he told Baldwin as their first session began, making the tennis ball sound like a woman's erogenous zones. 'Easy back, easy through.' He was used to working with unco-ordinated, bloated captains of industry and the pleat-skirted women who loved them, people for whom mere contact with the ball was an achievement. After looping a few facile forehands, Baldwin increased the tempo of the rally, penetrating deep into the back-court with crisply struck, top-spin missiles. Frank had to run hard to stay in the point, and when Baldwin advanced to the net, tried to lob him. The ball slowed at the top of its arc before a gust of wind sapped its momentum altogether and blew it back towards the net. When it plopped meekly into the service box, Baldwin bludgeoned it fiercely and squarely at Frank.

'Son of a bitch!' yelled Frank, diving to avoid the perfectly timed smash. 'What happened to *you* as a child?' There was a brutality in the way Baldwin played that was terrifying. Frank completed the initial twelve lessons Crawford had paid for, setting the ball machine to increasingly menacing speeds, and in the process honing Baldwin's return game. Then he concocted an excuse about the Olympic Club barring him from coaching non-members and disappeared.

In 1997, not long after Hong Kong's metamorphosis into a Special Administrative Region, Crawford and Anita made their one and only trip to see Baldwin. The trio spent a weekend at San Francisco's St Regis, hardly leaving the hotel after Anita contracted food poisoning the first night.

'What about your future?' Crawford asked Baldwin, over Sunday-morning brunch.

'I know you want me to start with the company,' said Baldwin. 'But I thought I might stay on here for a bit.'

'Ridiculous,' said Anita. 'Doing what?'

'A lot of my classmates are taking jobs with dotcoms.'

'Dot whats?' Anita said.

'Dotcoms, Ma. Computers, the Internet. Surely you've heard of the Internet?'

'Of course I have,' said Anita unconvincingly. 'Unacceptable. The plan has always been for you to come home.'

'I realise that, but listen. Pa, the future of our sales is online. We could grow the business tenfold, go truly global.'

'Funny,' Crawford said. 'Benson Lau brought up the same thing at our directors' meeting last month. I'm not sure. Our main customers are older. People like your mother,' he said looking at Anita. 'No offence, dear.'

'If I could just work here a few years, I'll come back with so much knowledge. The opportunities are amazing. And I know it'll help us down the track.'

'Baldwin,' Crawford said, tapping his right index finger on the table purposefully. 'I appreciate your enthusiasm, and you've done very well out here. But now's not the time for experiments.'

'It's not an experiment. People are making fortunes. Have you seen the NASDAQ?'

'Baldwin,' Anita said. 'Look your father in the eye.' She had caught him staring at his croissant, his thoughts drifting elsewhere. 'This is serious.'

'You will spend a year shadowing me,' Crawford said, his finger still keeping time like a metronome. 'Learn the business top to toe. I want you to come to dinners with clients and suppliers. Visit Shenzhen with me and learn about the factories. You can do things your way one day.'

'Are you listening?' said Anita. 'This is called common sense.' She seemed most pleased with the Shenzhen part of Crawford's plan, not so much for the work experience it would afford Baldwin, but because it meant maybe her husband wasn't having a mainland affair after all. At least not one he needed to hide from the family.

'You will gradually be given more responsibility,' Crawford said. 'In six, seven years from now, who knows, maybe you'll be ready to take over.'

'Really?' said Baldwin.

'Absolutely.'

This was how Crawford operated. Always seeming reasonable, as if he wanted only the best for his son. Baldwin knew he was outmaneuvered, at least for now.

'Chubby DiMarco's quite a character,' Baldwin said, not wanting to dwell on his predetermined future. He wanted to say *Chubby DiMarco's a dick*, but family meals like these were never occasions for speaking one's mind.

'If only you played golf,' Crawford said. 'I'd make you a director tomorrow.'

## IV. Backhands and Forehands

When Baldwin returned to Hong Kong in 1998, he landed at the new airport in Chek Lap Kok. Somewhere over the Pacific, he had jotted notes about his vision for the company: online sales, global marketing, and a host of other Stanford-inspired strategies he knew Crawford would never abide. At one point, he wrote the words *the son also rises*—not just a lame pun, he quickly realised, but a lame hope as well: Crawford showed no signs of retiring.

Underwhelmed by the top, toe, and everything in between of the family company, but with no other option than to stay the course, Baldwin dedicated the remainder of his twenties to tennis. So disciplined was he about practice that he missed the telecast of Leslie Cheung's memorial service in April 2003 after the founding father of Cantopop committed suicide. He helped the Colonial Club win no fewer than seven premierships and was named Athlete of the Year twice. As Crawford had predicted, Baldwin's imperious ground strokes gained him the respect of everyone in the clubhouse.

He started wearing a pirate-like bandanna, a tribute to then-number-one Andre Agassi. He had read on the Internet that the Las Vegan had grown up with the same cranial deformity he had, although since Agassi was dating Brooke Shields, Baldwin doubted the claim. He figured it was posted by a neurotic mother from somewhere like Spokane, Washington, who thought that by wantonly branding Andre with the same condition as her child, she could alleviate some of her guilt about smoking during pregnancy. Even still, the bandanna stayed. It had the same effect as Baldwin's high school swim cap, protecting him from the sideways sniggers of those more symmetrical than him. With it on, he could serve and volley an opponent into submission, whilst simultaneously displaying the grace of Baryshnikov. When he took it off, however—say for a steam bath with the boys—all his self-loathing returned. He wondered if his team-mates joked about him when he wasn't there.

'Great play today, Prince,' they'd say. Ever since Crawford had appeared on the cover of *Hong Kong C.E.O.* next to the caption 'The King of Cosmetics', this had been Baldwin's nickname at the club. 'How do you get that top-spin?'

'Got to have strong wrists,' Baldwin would say.

'Strong wrists,' came the inevitable innuendo. 'We know how you get *them*.'

There were end-of-season trips to Macau. Before the ferry had left Hong Kong waters, the boys were already trading tales of sexual conquests.

'What about you, Prince?' they'd ask.

Over time, Baldwin had perfected his stories. 'There was this one girl at Stanford,' he'd say, almost believing it, 'from Albuquerque, New Mexico. Tattoos, clit ring. Wildest sex I ever had.'

On Baldwin's thirtieth birthday, Crawford anointed him VP of the company. It was a small gesture, reported in a small article in the *Post*.

'There might have been a photo,' said Anita, midway through dinner at the Four Seasons, 'if you were married.'

'Anita,' Crawford said. 'Enough. I was thirty-nine when I married you.'

'That was different. You had girlfriends before me. Baldwin has no one.'

'I find that hard to believe,' Crawford said, winking at his son. 'Right, Baldwin?'

Crawford assumed, or at least hoped, that on Baldwin's jaunts to Macau, he'd sampled the city's brothels and massage parlours. He didn't know his son always snuck away, making an excuse to his team-mates about an early ferry to Hong Kong the next morning. He certainly didn't know that Baldwin was still a virgin, petrified more than anything of women who'd slept with other men. Prostitutes? Baldwin was fearful of them *especially*.

'I'm waiting for my stock to rise even higher,' said Baldwin.

'We're *all* waiting,' said Anita, before adjourning to the smoker's terrace.

No matter his achievements, the absence of a female partner was always at the forefront of Baldwin's thoughts. He dreamed of a world in which he could grow old with someone who didn't simply want him for his money. He stared into his shark-fin soup and told himself that such a world was pure fantasy.

## V. Too Many Weddings and a Funeral

At thirty-one, Baldwin sold the Happy Valley apartment he'd bought during SARS for triple its purchase price, then threw himself into his work. New product lines were launched in Australia, with Crawford reluctantly handing Baldwin responsibility for half of them. It meant he was required multiple times a week in Shenzhen. He hated the place, with its chintzy banquet halls and sleazy KTV joints. Unlike his father, who in the eighties endured arduous border crossings and maintained an apartment there, Baldwin simply took the car service, rarely staying overnight.

One afternoon, having just re-entered Hong Kong, Baldwin was dozing in and out of sleep as the green pixels of the New

Territories whirred by.

'It's your father,' Anita said on the phone. 'He has cancer.'

'How bad?' Baldwin asked the doctor, an hour later.

'It's already spread,' he was told, 'from the lungs to other organs. There are treatment options, but he may not last the year.'

'You see,' said Anita a month on, as Crawford recuperated at home after chemo. 'I told you many times to quit smoking. You never listen.'

Crawford deteriorated quickly. He was moved into palliative care, and as he wheezed his way toward death, Baldwin confronted a myriad of emotions. First, there was guilt—at keeping a journal of all the mistakes he believed his father had made with the company, at visiting a fortune teller to ask when this very moment of generational change would arrive. Then heartbreak for Anita, whose existence for the last thirty-six years had been defined entirely in relation to her husband. Finally, fear. The fear wore Baldwin down the most, more than any sense of grief or loss. In less than a year, he realised, maybe sooner, he would be thrust into the spotlight as the new face of Forever Jeune. Was he ready to wear Crawford's crown as Asia's 'King of Cosmetics'? Would his misshapen head even fit such a thing? He imagined the photo they'd publish in the *Post*. There he'd be, with his crag-like forehead, the butt-end of the Wong dynasty. Karma's way of evening up his family's long run of genetic advantage. As in high school, he longed to be invisible, hidden behind goggles and a swim cap.

Months passed, with the patriarch surrounded nightly by the extended family. Baldwin reconnected with the daughters of Archibald and Horatio, all but one of whom had married.

'Look at Baldwin,' Anita regularly complained. The old man was unresponsive, but it didn't stop her; the others were as much her audience as him. 'He's older than all of you, yet still not married. How can an unmarried man run a company like this?'

One day, in the smoker's courtyard of the hospital, Baldwin broke. 'What do you expect, Ma?' he said. 'All through high school, you say no girlfriends. College, the same. Now I'm working sixteen hours a day to keep this company running, and you complain about my marital status?'

'I want you to be happy,' Anita said. 'What's wrong with that?'

'What you want is to be the centre of attention at a stupid, fancy wedding. To boast to all your friends about how you set poor, hapless Baldwin up with his bride. Look at me, Ma.' He pulled his hair into a topknot, baring his forehead. 'Maybe I'm unmarried for a reason. Why can't you see that?'

She stubbed out her cigarette, weighing her response. Inhaled, exhaled. 'Daddy will be wondering where we are,' she said.

'Daddy doesn't know where *he* is.'

He wanted to hurt her, but Anita knew how to play tough. 'We'll talk about this later,' she said, calmly, then walked back into the hospital.

Crawford hung on for another nine months. Baldwin provided him daily updates on the latest sales figures and trends. 'Taiwan's doing well,' he'd say, even though it wasn't. Or, 'Still not happy with the website,' even though it was the most profitable part of the business. This was filial piety, Wong style.

When Crawford died, the family purchased a quarter-page ad in the *Post* to honour his achievements. Flags at no fewer than seven of Hong Kong's clubs flew at half-mast. Anita mourned for a month, before returning to the unfinished discussions of the courtyard.

'You're mid-thirties now,' she said, after her tour of Baldwin's new apartment. (Not long ago, she had called herself mid-forties, until Crawford outed her with a lavish, surprise fiftieth.) 'I won't be made a laughing stock,' she said. 'You are going to find someone young and pretty. Someone like I was for Daddy.'

This meant *she* was going to find Baldwin someone young and pretty, or at least someone better looking than him. He wouldn't stop her. As much as it pained him, he knew this was his best chance. He may now have been, after banking his inheritance cheque, millions of US dollars more eligible. But he owned countless more insecurities than securities. 'What do you propose?' he said.

Anita explained that most of her yacht/cricket/racquet club friends' daughters were already married. Fortunately, Hong Kong abounded with ambitious families of slightly lower social status, families one or two frames out of the social pages at the moment, but nonetheless on the way up. Anita knew this because she herself had grown up in an aspirational family, a mere tax bracket above middle class. 'Who knows what would have happened,' she often said, 'if I hadn't met Crawford.'

A series of dates with the daughters of such families was arranged. Try as he might, Baldwin was hopeless under these conditions. He may have learned, under Crawford's stewardship, how to host a business lunch, but as for real dates, he'd never been on one. Not surprisingly, they all went disastrously, no matter how much pressure the girls were under from their parents to find chemistry with Baldwin.

On one date, Baldwin nearly kissed a waify girl called Pixie Chan, whom all night he had plied with alcohol. It was the closest he'd gotten to first base since Laurie from Albuquerque, and fittingly, the girl's breath again smelled boozy. Right before their wine-stained lips met, Pixie noticed the scar behind Baldwin's hairline. 'What's that?' she asked.

'What's what?' Baldwin said, his whole body tensing. He suddenly felt sober.

'This,' Pixie said, reaching up to Baldwin's forehead. She pushed back his hair and gently stroked the scar. 'This.'

He let her linger there, just for a bit, feeling the transfer of energy between them. Then he seized her wrist, gripping it so hard she began to cry.

'I'm sorry,' he said, releasing her. 'I'm sorry.'

'What did I do?' she asked.

Baldwin stared at the footpath. He wanted to stay, make things right. But all he could say was, 'I should go,' before retreating into the night.

In the cab home, Baldwin tried to make sense of the force that had possessed him and made him hurt Pixie. He replayed all the usual horror scenes: the schoolyard beltings at Saint Augustine's, the wretchedness of his college dorm room. He decided that his was a head only a mother could love. The next morning, when he told Anita that none of the dates were going well, she looked at him with such disappointment that he wondered if even *she* could love him.

'Sales have rebounded in Taiwan,' he said, desperate to change the subject. 'New figures from the mainland are promising too.'

'What do I care about the mainland?' she said. 'I'll be sixty soon.' (Anita could inflate as well as deflate her age depending on the emotive effect she desired.)

Age was never an issue for Baldwin. When he pictured life with a spouse, he always imagined the two of them as old. Old people doing old-people things: walking along foreshores, reading newspapers across from each other over dim sum. No more were Baldwin's dreams pornographic: no nakedness, no flesh, no youth. Being Baldwin Wong did that you.

There were still many others in Hong Kong saying 'I do'. For the next year, Baldwin assumed Crawford's place alongside Anita at Saturday weddings. This interfered with his tennis schedule, and before a record eighth premiership could be won, he stood down from the team. Again—filial piety.

The weddings were always the same. Always someone like Veronica Mui's youngest daughter marrying some lawyer or doctor. Always people making 'ooh' noises when the marshmallow bride walked down the aisle. Always Baldwin going home solo at the end of the night, too tired to masturbate, too numb to cry.

Neither Anita nor Baldwin took pleasure in gifting *lai see* to the happy couples. Both knew that at his age, in his position, it should have been Baldwin and a wife handing out the red envelopes, not some lady who'd soon be sixty.

Then the weddings abruptly stopped. Maybe his mother's prophecy was coming true, and there were simply no more singles left to be married.

'Maybe I should give up,' she told him one afternoon. He wasn't sure if she was playing games or being genuine. 'I've done my best. You seem perfectly capable of ruining your own life.'

At this point in the story, Baldwin could have returned to the tennis courts, seeking asylum once more in sport. With a drop shot newly introduced to his game, that eighth premiership was surely within Baldwin's reach. Likewise he could have immersed himself in his work, setting about overhauling Forever Jeune's operations the way he'd always dreamed. Baldwin Wong pursued neither of these paths. Instead, he found God.

## VI. Salvation Street

But not right away.

During his series of Anita-approved dates, Baldwin had conducted some half-hearted research into other ways he might find someone young and pretty. After the particularly awkward evenings, the ones that ended with him pretending to be sick or manufacturing an excuse about an early trip to Shenzhen tomorrow—definitely after the date with Pixie—he would go home and type combinations of words like *dating, companionship,* and *virgin* into Google. He gave up when he was redirected one too many times to porn sites, but before this, in 2009, he'd been motivated enough to create a Word document, bulleting the various options.

With Anita now announcing her retirement from matchmaking (although he doubted whether she was serious), he revisited the file. There was speed dating, which he'd ruled out on grounds that timed conversations of six minutes, terminated by a bell, were probably not optimal conditions for a man riddled with self-doubt. Then there were online dating sites, which usually required the account holder to post a recent photo of themselves; photographs had never been Baldwin's party trick, unless the party was Halloween, in which case he made a great monster. There were happy-ending massages, although ever since Sex Ed. with Brother O'Callaghan in Fourth Form, he'd been terrified of the clap. Finally, at the bottom of the list, was a word he had tried to expunge from his vocabulary since Saint Augustine's: *church.*

It came to back to him. One night, while searching for signs of life of Frank 'Chubby' DiMarco, he had stumbled across a website for Christian singles. (There were no were no fewer than seven Catholics called DiMarco, he'd discovered, who were looking for someone to love because He loved them first.) Scanning through the profile pics of the women, it had all made sense. *Church,* Baldwin thought. Of course. Where else was he going to meet his saviour?

He decided to resurrect the plan, to give church a chance. He phoned Jordan Ng, a new member of the Colonial Club who had worked for Lehman Brothers before the GFC, but was now a trainee pastor.

'I was thinking,' Baldwin said, once Jordan worked out who he was, 'we should play some tennis.'

Two days later, they were taking a post-game steam bath, Baldwin intermittently wiping his brow with his Andre Agassi bandanna. Jordan had turned out to be a very adroit player, with Baldwin prevailing only 7-6, 7-5. They touched on the subject of women, but not in the lurid detail that Baldwin's old team-mates preferred. Baldwin had no need for his well-practised fictions about girls-gone-wild he'd slept with at Stanford; Jordan was only interested in whether he wanted a 'life partner'.

'Do you think you'll get married?' he asked Baldwin.

'You know how it is,' Baldwin said.

'I do. It can be hard in this city.'

'I used to date a lot. But now I struggle to find the time.'

'You need to make time. Put your well-being first.'

'I was thinking about coming to church.'

'To meet someone? We're not exactly a dating agency.'

'No, I didn't mean that. I used to go at school, but I've fallen out of the habit. Ever since my father died, it's like I've lost my bearings.'

'Well, if you're hearing the call, I'd be happy to introduce you to Pastor Chad. He's our head preacher, the man who's training me. He runs sessions for newcomers on Tuesday nights.'

And so it passed that, on the next Tuesday, Baldwin attended his first bible study class at the United Followers of Christ Evangelical Church in Tin Hau. *The United Followers*: they sounded more like a football supporters' club than a congregation, and in a way, they were. The 'church' occupied two floors of a nondescript office block. There were no gothic spires or stone facades. When you exited the lift, you were immediately greeted by giant photos of the United Followers doing various Christian things: playing volleyball, building human pyramids on beaches, mountain-biking.

It was all very social, nothing like the interminable masses Baldwin had sat through at Saint Augustine's. Sometimes the group met at pubs to discuss their favourite scripture passages. They went on junk trips in summer. Once a month they had tennis night, which of course Baldwin starred at, although he sometimes let Jordan steal a set off him. Baldwin quickly became as committed a Christian as anyone there.

Pastor Chad was a spry man from Southern California. He ran half-marathons, never drank full-fat milk, and sported a ponytail into his fifties. He was a whiz on the electric guitar. Instead of dreary hymns, Chad led the United Followers in power ballads about the Holy Ghost and a thing called The Word. The more he opened his heart to the Word, Baldwin slowly began to let go of his demons. Brick by brick, he built a wall of belief that maybe love for him was possible, one day, if God's will decreed it. 'Listen to The Word,' Chad would say in his sermons, elongating the word 'Word'. 'The Word is your salvation.' In his second month of weekly attendance, Baldwin was invited into Chad's office for a private conference.

'Unhappy you are,' Chad began, a little Yoda-like. He turned over a sheet of legal pad that bore the logo of the firm he had worked for in LA. 'This,' he said, drawing a straight line with his pacer, 'this is the road trip of life.' Beneath that he drew another line, which halfway along he steered upward so that the two lines crossed. 'And this,' he said, tapping their point of intersection, 'is what happens when we find a soulmate.' Baldwin appreciated the way Pastor Chad explained the obvious both verbally *and* visually. 'Are you free for lunch tomorrow?'

'I was thinking of going for a swim. Why?'

'I organise a monthly gathering of our younger members. Mostly we go for a meal, sometimes a hike up the Peak. There's someone I'd very much like you to meet.'

'Does he play tennis?'

'Her name's Hilary Tan,' Pastor Chad said, savouring all four syllables of her name. 'And she's beautiful.'

In the past, Baldwin's mind would have flooded with questions. Since when did this man of devotion, he would have asked, this buyer of organic produce, this *Chad*, transform from preacher to pimp? Who was he to look at poor, hapless Baldwin and decide he needed a soulmate? He had a mother for that, thank you very much. Who was Pastor Chad working for? Where did he get off?

'It's like he's trying to set me up,' Baldwin told Jordan Ng after class.

'Pastor Chad thinks only of others,' said Jordan. 'If he says you should meet her, what have you got to lose?'

The following day, Baldwin arrived with nothing to lose at the busy *cha chaan teng* Pastor Chad had selected. There, he met Hilary Tan, twenty-three, a slightly cross-eyed MBA student from HKUST. Later, he would learn that she had a habit of not moving her arms when she walked, but presently, he fell in love with her heart-shaped face. It made her seem gentle and caring. He decided over Hong Kong-style French toast that this was a woman he could marry. Baldwin was now exactly half the age Crawford had been when he died. If he didn't secure a co-pilot for his road trip with Christ now, then when? Then who?

Of course, by the time the pineapple buns were on the table, Baldwin was already back to being Baldwin. He imagined Hilary a decade from now, waking beside him and suddenly realising how much better she could have done. He saw her running off to London with some banker with a cleft chin called Hamish. He saw her growing bored of the privileges afforded to members of no fewer than seven Hong Kong clubs. He saw her discovering more sensual pleasures than those either he or The Word could offer.

That night, Baldwin called his mother.

'Why do you tell me this now?' she said. 'I have no one to enjoy it with.'

'Are we still on for Saturday?' Baldwin said. He'd promised to take her to the movies.

'Nothing worth seeing,' said Anita. 'Not a single decent one.'

Hours later, Baldwin couldn't sleep. He stared at his curtains through the flickering light from the television. He tried to imagine Hilary beside him, wondered if she was doing the same. He was already sketching the story of the troubled adulthood of Baldwin Wong, the story still to come. He realised it was Hilary, not himself, who was risking it all.

# SAVING GRACE
Ploy Pirapokin

Picture this: I was standing in the back of Tribeka, a sprawling circus-themed nightclub. Grime and garage tunes enveloped me like they would in an underground tavern. I was with my best mate Chris on one side and my other best mate Greg on the other, all hoping to pass for eighteen. I was looking Chinese chavvy-chic, wobbling in five-inch platform pumps and wearing a bustier stuffed with cotton pads. The boys looked like pikey princes, identically twinned in too-baggy jeans and T-shirts with Zoo York graffitied across their chests. Chris's jet-black bangs parted to cover his large brown puppy-dog eyes, braces barely hidden under his thin lips.

We played the part of the British working-class youth, a tribute to our idols in *Little Britain* on Star TV. It was ten past eleven and we were waiting for a text message from Smitty to make a move. Greg held up a gin and tonic for me. His six-foot-five frame convinced the bartender he was of age.

'So I totally had a wank last night but was tired and just wrapped up the jizzy tissue in more tissue and left it by my bed,' he said. 'Went for breakfast in the morning, came back, and found my poor mum had tidied it up.'

I gagged. 'That's disgusting.'

Greg wiggled his tongue at me.

'Guys,' Chris shot us a warning look. 'Stay focused.'

'We've been here for more than half an hour! And there's no weed or fit girls, just a bunch of corpses rolling,' Greg protested.

'How much are we trying to make tonight?' I asked Chris.

'Just enough.'

At fifteen, Chris, Greg, and I had already mastered the life of an undercover agent: A-grade students by day, ketamine dealers by night. Greg got the liquid kizzo from our dealer near the border, double-boiled the crap out of it, gave it to Chris who then ground it into a white crusty residue. I took it in powder form in vials to the clubs with a fake ID that said that I was a Filipina named Bianca. We'd sell enough bags for money to buy shoes, bags, clothes—things we could've easily gotten from our parents but things we'd rather say we got ourselves. We wanted accessories, didn't need necessities. We took risks and did everything in the extreme when we were high. When we studied, we studied all night to get that A, scribbling the answers on our thighs in blue ink and sipping cough syrup to numb the come-down. We'd shoot hoops until five in the morning and walk into school immaculately dressed in our beige uniforms and shiny leather shoes. We'd skip class to smoke shisha and have lunch at the Peninsula dressed in wife-beaters and sandals. We dined *al fresco* at *dai pai dongs*, making racist and politically incorrect jokes about everybody around us. We'd sniff and smoke ketamine, mix it in our drinks, then I'd put on a puppet show where pens and glue sticks talked, moved, and ate each other. We split our sides guffawing: when we laughed, we laughed like it was the end of the world. What the fuck was moderation? We never did anything halfway.

Only that night we weren't going all the way, we were going *past* all the way. We were trying to sell K at a nightclub we'd never been to. Situated next to the Grand Hyatt hotel in Wan Chai, this privileged playground with two stages and a caged dance floor had waitresses performing raunchy choreographed shows throughout the night. This island of sexy silliness in the sea of karaoke bars, seedy bathhouses, and rent-by-the-hour motels had a fiendishly strict door policy. We would barely have made it through the wooden double-doors if we hadn't been on Smitty's guest list.

Our boy, Smit, connected us. He had told us that there'd be people here interested in playing Casper. But we knew this club belonged to Alex O'Neal and his mates.

'Let me tell you about him,' Smitty once said to us after class, jammed in the corner table of our local Tai Hing, the only true *cha chaan teng* coffee shop left. 'You don't mess with Alex O'Neal.'

How do I even begin to explain Alex O'Neal? A high school drop-out, a thoroughbred, he'd bust out of street bars, pupils dilated, chatting away about nothing, a tribal dragon on the forearm he'd put around a gaggle of young girls with mosquito-bite breasts poking their oversized dresses. He broke his own dad's nose after the old man refused to give him money. When kids ran away from home, he would be the last to see them. One time, I saw him loitering around MTR exits at closing time, dragging a cracked cricket bat beside him, swearing. Truth is, we knew of him. We'd never met the guy. We'd never wanted to.

'Last year, he got this girl pregnant,' Smitty continued, leaning over the dirty plastic table. 'She was in year eight. Fourteen. She told him and he wasn't very happy.'

'Why didn't she just get an abortion?' I asked, doling out the four cups of milk tea that arrived. 'Where did she go to school?'

'German Swiss.'

'What did she do with the baby?' Greg asked.

'She committed suicide.'

'No way.'

'That's sad, man.'

'Well, everyone thought she did,' Smitty slurped his frothy beverage. 'But then we found out that Alex was at her house on the day she fell down eleven storeys. She had fallen through the screens.'

Greg, Chris and I avoided eye contact.

\*

Greg was my best friend first. I liked him because he had a British accent. The damn British accent. Anyone who knows me knows that I absolutely love talking *faux* British. In my own mind, I've perfected it. That's what four years of international school does to you: it teaches you to speak English fluently like the colonialists. I had hopped into the elevator to get to art class when Greg, eleven, pale as clay and the only white guy in my class, walked closely behind. When we were standing side by side, I turned and blurted, 'Halloi!' He looked straight at me with dying hazel eyes.

I grinned sheepishly and looked down.

We became friends that humid September. Greg always waited for me at the bottom of the slide in the quads. I liked the way his dark blond hair opposed my inky strands as I slid straight into his stomach. Playgrounds turned into hand fumbling movie dates into sneaking in kisses while we wandered down our six-hundredth jewellery store in Ocean Terminal and before we could count the years, I saw how my first name sounded so good next to his last name. Everyone knew I was his girl. There wasn't anywhere we didn't go together.

I met Chris through Greg. They were on the same school bus. He was the new kid in school: a small, leather-hued Thai boy with large protruding eyes. He became the guest star to our twosome, always roping us in on the fun. We had been waiting for Greg to get out of his Chemistry tutoring session outside the Festival Walk mall, and after an hour of sucking on menthol cigarettes and blowing smoke into large air ventilators stacked like bookshelves down the sidewalk, we decided to try K for the first time. In a doorway, Chris pulled out a stolen pill from his older brother, Eli, to share.

'It'll make you smile, Jax.'

We weren't stupid. We knew drugs were bad. But all these stuck-up morals and 'should-nots' fall to the side when you take your first hit. You forget all about that because you know how damn good it makes you feel. The first K-punch only needs a couple of minutes to settle in your veins and heaven lasts only up to four hours. At first your eyes begin to water; the tips of your lashes vibrate on the tops of your cheeks. Your lips spread apart as if they were being smoothed to the back of your face, exposing your wet gums and smooth enamels to the air. Your breath quickens, and you inhale deeper, sucking in your soul as you rise through your eyeballs above your body like an angel looking down at yourself from above. The air becomes peppery, prickling your arms, and your nose slightly dribbles from the chilling vibrations. Energy pours out from the top of your head, trickles down to your weightless legs. Your tongue battles creamy metallic saliva foaming under the roof of your mouth. There's no need to communicate. Take a joke and imagine roaring with laughter until tears well up uncontrollably, rim-job your eyelashes, and drip off your chin. Take an orgasm and multiply that by a thousand watts, all the clenching and unclenching when you're at the brink and just about to bust. *For every atom belonging to me as good belongs to you.* You suspend your self, and your senses become alert and alive. You become earthed in your essence, inhabit another self, and give it life for a while. Individuality seems to dissolve into boundless being. Death becomes a laughable impossibility.

'Feel it yet?' Chris asked, eyeing me warily.

I agreed and slowly nodded, as if my chin waded through molasses to meet my chest. I slumped down. His gaze was detached, but he held onto me. I was excited that he could be so important so quickly. I didn't have a drug addiction—I had a risk addiction. I wanted to live my life free from anxiety and insecurities.

Tongues melted as one slippery eel. I led him hand-in-hand across the marble floors like a crocodile of school children. We stopped underneath the McDonald's sign, lights pulsating above us, lids shut and noses grazing. What did it all mean? Everything. Nothing. We didn't care—we laughed and ordered another Happy Meal. Greg caught up with us later, watched our eyes diluting in silence.

The three of us strolled to the train station that afternoon without exchanging a single word. Our parents were waiting for us to come home from our afterschool activity. Cars purred on the streets, stopping as waves of people piled onto the yellow zebra crossings, engrossed in droning chatter. Garbage collectors swept cigarette butts and plastic drink cartons off the pavements as Greg seemingly separated himself from Chris and me like a betrayed husband.

We quickly shoved aside this incident, crammed it into the back drawers of our minds. Moving forward, them and me, just us three.

\*

So here we were now, deep in Alex O'Neal's domain, fancier than the alleyways, the house scenes and the rented lofts we were used to. The music was your standard dance-your-pants-off non-stop mix. There were manicured feet bouncing in improbable heels. Pockets of snogging on the dance floor. Pawing by the loos. In the booth directly in front of us, a tall male model was trying to lick the hand of an enormous drag queen in a headdress of blood-red feathers.

Green pokeballs, blue Armanis, double-stacked yellow Mickey Mouses, and every single kind of ecstasy pill were sold there. Kids didn't want K when they could roll. We knew our customers well: the I-bankers, the locals in band-four loser schools, and the occasional adventurous tourist. But not the international kids who snuck out on Friday nights to Tribeka. K is not something you do at a club to get your grind on.

We needed Smit's help to break into the international-school-kid crowd. After all, expat kids are rich and while we were expat kids, we didn't have the same amount of pull he had. (As an expat, you own more than one passport. You've probably flown in first class before your thirteenth birthday. Your parents are usually in the government or global banks, and they've been photographed for the *Forbes* Richest People in Asia annual story. You have two homes and a yacht.) Expat kids became our new target market, and we knew we would hit it big with these bored international kids and their deep pockets. We would have to make it through the five British high schools first: Island School, South Island, West Island, Sha Tin, and our own, Queen Elizabeth the Second. Saturate the market. Make sure the adventurous ones talked about their greatest K high during football matches, drama conferences, and in classes so that more kids wanted in.

In Psych class, we struck our first deal with Smitty, son of a diamond miner and part of the Indian political family. Like black ore, his parents' influence seeped through the cracks of civilised democratic hearings, green notes paving a road for his future. With him on our side, we went unnoticed, booking hotel rooms for our all-night binges, customers coming and going like a dumb waiter. If Greg, Chris, and I were the dealers, Smitty was the vibe ambassador, making sure everyone who came through the door let their inhibitions go, ready to tumble down the K-hole. He wanted in on the fun. He was the first and last person you saw at the door, while Greg, Chris, and I lurked in the background, pretending to be party-goers who happened to have the goods. Our parents trusted we were studying together, attending child-like slumber parties, and celebrating weeklong Diwali festivities.

'You revised those Cognitive Psych notes?' I once asked, taking my seat next to him.

'What about it?'

'Bandura's theory?'

'Bobo dolls?'

'Yeah, learned violent behaviour.'

'Learning new things every day,' Smitty concluded, handing me a pirated copy of a movie, *Lock, Stock and Two Smoking Barrels*. We believed he was untouchable.

Our sales pitch was simple: Got money? Buy from us. Got money, no game? Buy from us. Don't want involvement with the triads? You know Smit's not a hoodrat. Need a place to get high? We got options. Scared of your parents? They'll never find out. Ours were never home, and when they were, mine were too preoccupied with making sure I was clean, fed, and busy. We'd schedule a pick-up when they were off on month-long business trips to China or some place foreign.

Don't fall for amateur move number one: getting drugs at the club from randos. You can get horse tranquilliser instead of K and won't be able to tell the difference in the dark. But at least you'd have already heard of Smit and his family.

Amateur move number two: OD-ing on too much K and hallucinating through the streets. We don't want bodies leading back to us up the uneven, cemented tiles of Lan Kwai Fong. We've got your back, and we'll make sure you get on the twenty-four hour bus home.

My parents, bless them, never asked me much to know what was going on.

'We're trapped,' Chris once said to Greg and me after school in my bedroom, his back on my Ralph Lauren paisley printed blanket.

'Tell that to the butcher in the wet market.'

'No, I'm serious, Jax. We're put up on this pedestal. Like, made to feel good about all these opportunities we have over other people. All these advantages.'

We paid more for our high-school tuition than people did for college. Our allowances were more than a person made at their first entry-level job.

I spun to face him, soaking in my space: a French-style antique dresser topped with a large white mirror and drawers filled to the brim with my make-up. Gold-trimmed wallpaper lined the all-cream carpeted bedroom. Platinum picture frames hung on the walls, holding my two tiny parents. There was a photo of us in front of the Louvre in Paris, my stern-faced father with a solid, stoic line for a smile and my buxom-cheeked mother with bouncy hair blown back by a breeze. The same parents who wanted a pretty and docile daughter with the perfect hair, a good job, a family, a TV, a house, and health insurance. Both were hugging a petite version of me, a tanned girl with waist-long hair in a puffed-up red winter jacket sulkily staring at the photographer.

'I wouldn't trade it for anything in the world,' Greg murmured.

We knew all about this safe and secure life, Chris, Greg, and me: son of the man who brought cable TV to the whole of Asia, son of the British Ambassador to Hong Kong, and daughter of a real-estate mogul. Poor little rich kids who had everything mapped out. I was born into a family of two over-protective parents. Sent when I was six to a private school where French-immersion trips were held in the Alps. Had a penthouse apartment with floor-to-ceiling windows to call home and Ballantyne cashmere sweaters to wear when it got cold. I had a life that many kids did not. Was I ungrateful? Maybe. But why would I want to choose what I already knew? I wasn't looking forward to having responsibility; to earning honest, legal money; to making an effort to be normal. It was never a choice between my perfect childhood or being the bad girl. It was never about whether or not selling ketamine was a bad thing. There was a demand, and I was the supply. Getting the grades and the K was just too easy. I was taking a risk, wasn't I? I was getting what I wanted from both ends of the spectrum without anyone else but the three of us knowing what was going on.

Still, we never saw any way out.

\*

The crowd was a pick'n'mix of postcodes, colour, gender, sexuality, and age. The bass vibrated underneath our feet as we stood rooted to the mirrors reflecting the staccato disco lights next to a huddle of suits and miniskirts waiting in line for the loo.

Chris had been mad texting for the past two hours, fingers furiously punching the numbers on his Motorola flip-phone.

'Fuck, Jax. Alex is coming here tonight,' He turned and showed me a text from Smitty.

*He's coming with backup.*

I spat out my gin and tonic. 'With what?'

'Backup dancers. Pretty pink ballerinas.'

I tiled my head, eyes wide.

'His fucking crew, you idiot.'

'Then we gotta get out of here.' I slapped Greg on his shoulder and started towards the exit behind the caged dance floor.

Greg halted. 'How did Alex know we'd be coming?'

'I have no idea.' I kept pushing Greg through small groups of club-goers gyrating to the music, slinking by moving bodies as we inched closer to freedom.

Chris paused as if he was thinking of something calming to say.

'It's dodgy, this whole thing.'

'Well, I trust Smit.' I tried to get everyone in the right brain space. 'He's never brought us anywhere we couldn't unload.'

We walked straight into a brown bulging body.

'Last person I thought I'd see,' Chris growled. 'Smit fucking Gupta.'

Smitty grinned nervously, his smile taking over the bottom half of his face. His dark curls slicked back with pomade that smelled like cardamom, the whites in his eyes prominent against his smooth, ebony skin.

'I thought I gave you stupid-heads a fair warning.'

'You told us to get here at ten-thirty with three kilos and then you show up a good two hours later!' Chris said, pushing me out of the way.

Smitty cast a look over his shoulder, hunched down and reached for us to group up.

'Look, Alex believes there are outsiders on his turf. Your best bet is to scram.'

Chris bristled. 'What about the stash?'

'Just give me the stuff and I'll get you guys back.'

'Get us back with what?'

'How do you know about Alex?' I asked. This questioned seemed like a double-edged sword.

Smitty froze.

'You'll have to pay us for it then,' Chris said solemnly.

I nodded. Smitty didn't need to take our stash. One, it's a hop, skip, and shuffle across the border where K-jai is so easily available, coming in odourless bulk quantities, stuffed in printer-ink cartridges and charcoal bags hauled back on the KCR into Hong Kong. Two, it's cheap to manufacture, produced legally by veterinary sources as an alternative to angel dust used to resuscitate patients, then passed through the gaps of corrupt fingers like sand, diffused through social pipes of triads, gangs of unemployed basketball players, and retired taxi drivers holed up in their rabbit-cage bedrooms.

*

In fact, he could always come with us when we met up our dealer, Fa'a Yu, a local kid, product of a low-banded Chinese-medium school, his opportunities limited by the one exam he took at sixteen to determine his place. Nobody had noticed that he had become an orphan at a young age and had no time to study while supporting himself running a squalid noodle stall.

I had met him by volunteering to teach English to local students from a nearby all-Chinese school. Sporting dreads, a mean squint, and a lean androgynous frame, he spent the first weeks of class standing at the back, disgusted that a third-culture kid like me deserved respect. At the end of our fourth session, he strolled up to me and said, 'Wanna sing-K after class with us?'

So maybe it was my fault that K came into our lives. After all, it was my decision to enter the blue-lighted building. The walls were covered in posters advertising the neighbouring, gentlemen-only, 24-hour saunas. We took a rickety shoebox lift to the second floor, where Fa'a negotiated a private room for us to sing pop songs.

He stopped to take out fine, white crystalline powder, packed in a small, transparent, resealable plastic bag. 'You don't mind? They want it.'

The other kids swarmed him like krill to a whale's mouth. A quick pop to the brain, a poor man's cocaine, it's the local drug of choice. So easily consumed, not physically addictive. If there were capital punishment for possessing, trafficking, and snorting K, only then would we stop.

The city is awash with ketamine.

Finally, Smitty said, 'I'll give you two hundred dollars. You need to get rid of it, right?'

I stepped back, holding Greg and Chris next to me. 'That's not even a fair price!'

I'm glad I didn't launch myself at him because the next thing you know, the lights came on, blinding everyone. Girls hid their faces behind their hands, squealing. Guys jumped behind the thin wooden balustrades separating the tables, behind layers of champagne bottles strewn across cushions. A large group of tall tattooed guys appeared, sweeping aside hordes of clubbers. The music cut off. Pills fell, scattering across the floor like marbles. Heels scampered away and the crowd surged into every available nook to watch.

'What are you kids doing here?'

The robust voice came from the left of me. Alex O'Neal stood with ten of his henchmen between us and the caged dance floor, our getaway route. They were real men, adults with bulging arms and wide chests, their faces covered with hoodies, ski masks, and trucker hats. A wolf pack cornering their prey.

Alex stepped out front, his arms etched with tribal tattoos and a large dragon, the defining one, emblazoned on his forearm. His bleached white hair was spiked, his thick lips bruised and swollen probably from the last altercation. His eyes narrowed.

'Are you talking to us?' Greg said stepping out in front of me.

Greg was scrawny, ghostly in comparison to Alex.

'Are you stealing my customers?'

I looked at Chris and then at Greg. Alex looked back at his crew, increasing the torturous interrogation, a scowl at the ready. His face was rigid and he loomed over us.

'What are we, a Mexican gang now?' Greg asked in a sing-song tone. 'Want to throw your shoes up around the lamp post outside and claim your grounds?'

'Don't aggravate me. I know you three are here to sell K,' Alex said. 'Give me the kilo and I won't hand you over to the police. I know who you kids are. In fact, I won't even blackmail your parents with this. Oh that's right, you lot are scared shitless of what mummy and daddy would say.'

His crew begins to cat-call, holler, and whistle.

'We don't have anything,' I chimed in, stubbornly defiant.

'Watch your mouth, bitch, before I seal it up for you.'

Alex raised his hands, theatrically mimicked a swift back-handed slap.

Chris took hold of my arms, thumbs digging into the crooks of my elbows.

'Put a leash on her, mate.'

'We're not selling anything,' Greg said forcefully.

'My boy Smitty here,' Alex motioned at Smitty who looked away from us, 'told me you guys were going to hook it up with the K.'

There was awkward shuffling in the background as party-goers slowly trickled out. Bright ceiling lights emitted a low buzz. I held my breath. We could run, tackle Alex, then make a mad dash for the exit. Or pound towards the nearest one to us, throw the bags of K to the ground, and get out. Kick, shove, push, then sprint. Cut our losses.

If Greg was rattled by the furore, he didn't show it. Chris, on the other hand, looked as if he had just woken up from a coma.

'Smitty,' Greg said, shaking his head. 'What's in it for you, mate?'

'Now we're going to have some good shit to trip on tonight,' Alex nodded at Smitty. 'For free.'

'We're not selling anything,' Greg repeated. 'Apologies for the misunderstanding. I'm sorry we couldn't be of more help to you.'

Smitty squirmed reluctantly at the stressful, adrenaline-fuelled exchange between his new friends and us.

'I'll make you guys a deal,' Alex said.

Greg glared.

'Don't think your 'rents will care, do you? Well son, I have nothing to lose. I've been in the game a lot longer than you kids have been. You guys are playing mobster dress-up.'

The movie reeled: older versions of Greg, Chris, and me in black graduation cloaks, holding hands and laughing, exchanging pecks. London's Big Ben swayed, its bell silent, against a big black flame. A numbered list: *Get Married, First Baby,* and *First House* neatly checked off, crumpled.

'We'll be all right,' Greg said. 'You can put us in jail and we'll get out. You can even take us for ransom and we'll pay it off. And,' he looked directly at Alex, 'when my father buys Tribeka and all the little clubs you and your mates run around in, we'll see who's got nothing to lose.'

'You are a fucking joke,' Alex said.

I nodded at Chris, signalling defeat.

But Greg, brave, proud or mental, threw a punch at Alex, who ducked.

I screamed at him, '*Watch out!*'

Alex bellowed, grabbed Greg by the neck with one arm. 'I'm going to make you my little bitch.'

Greg's head swivelled like an office chair, chin hitting his shoulder from a blow.

Chris made an embarrassing yelp, his head smashed into the mirrored wall.

I spat at the nearest man, his big nose a lump under the ski mask, and kneed him in the stomach. I darted for the exit. A garbage bin lid cracked my head.

Last thing I saw was a San Miguel bottle, smashed against the bar, its broken end swiping Greg's face.

*

A high-pitched hum permeated my hearing; delicate antennae fluttered on my arm, brushing back baby hairs. I opened bloodshot eyes into fluorescent white. Flies circled me, hazy round motions like a child's science-project solar system. Greg's voice lifted me up from the pitch-black milieu, flipped the sirens, hit the lights in my brain, and I whimpered.

'Well, *avada kedavra*, you're up.'

Greg sat topless, holding his shirt, bloody and wet, mopping the spot where his left ear had been cut. It resembled a bleeding cauliflower sitting on a garden patch of dried blood, shards of glass, and dark blond hair. His face was hot, eyes swollen, and nose wet.

I started to cry.

'I'm so sorry, I'm so sorry Greg—'

'No, they didn't touch you.'

'Your ear, it's my fault, we should've left sooner—'

'I wouldn't have let them. Besides, it's not fun for them to take advantage of girls when they're unconscious.'

He sat with his head still balanced on one arm. Chris sat silently next to him, bruised eyes like ripe plums. For the past two hours, the two of them had hidden me in the truncated corners of this sepia-toned emergency room. Concrete frames in terrain-tangled pipes, buried under the weight of urban dross. The waiting room's stripped walls and rusty chairs sat still, uninviting and old. A small fan in the front of the room spun unevenly, every turn a double-bump beat. We were buried in the rubble against the peeling paint, amid the collecting dust of the crumbling, almost-abandoned clinic.

'Are you feeling better?' Greg winced. 'You were out for a while there.'

Globules of clotted blood formed a knotted mess that appeared to be growing on the left side of his head. He looked so vulnerable, his hazel eyes green under the lamps. I breathed slowly, rhythmically, trying to ignore the metallic smell from his face, like iodine was sweating out of his pores.

Feeling Greg meant I had no me to feel.

'I'm a little dizzy still.' He stopped to exhale drowsily.

'It's been cut, not cut off,' Chris added reassuringly. 'We'll get it cleaned up, get some antibiotics—'

'So we're going to stick with the story when my parents get back that it was a rugby scrimmage gone wrong?'

I conjured up a double-decker bus squishing us to our clean death. Much more pleasurable and preferable to facing our 'rents.

Chris shook his head, 'Our parents will never know. I told the police we were real drunk so they wouldn't report the assault.'

The police had shown up shortly after, Smitty having called them beforehand, playing the part of a concerned citizen. Said he was scared with all the noise going on across the street from the club. They followed the crowd and found us upstairs. Alex and his mates booked it.

'Does the side of your head look like a bloody Rwandan genocide?' That was Greg.

'They obviously knew we were lying,' Chris said.

'I don't trust that dickhead.'

'It's a government clinic, so we can pay out of our own pocket without having to register or get our parents' health insurance involved,' Chris pleaded with us. 'I don't trust him either, but he felt bad. Let him make it up to us.'

Greg refused to say a word. I saw his thoughts boil over.

'I hope Alex finds him before we do.'

Chris took out his phone, 'I'm going to give Eli a call to pick us up. That way, we don't have to walk out in broad bloody daylight like this to go home.'

He stood up and stormed off behind us for the toilets. Greg tilted his head and motioned for me to follow Chris to make sure our third musketeer wasn't upset.

'I was worried sick about you when I woke up, y'know.'

I shifted next to him. His hands were in mine.

'This is the most manly you've ever looked,' I said, smirking.

'You're a sicko, Jax. Did you know that?'

He rubbed my fingers feebly. 'I saw one of the guys hit you with a bin. What a fucking coward, knocking out a girl. I was pissed off. So I started knocking tables over and throwing bottles at whoever came at me—'

'We don't have to do this anymore,' I interjected. He bowed his head. The drenched shirt flopped in his hands.

'We bit off way more than we could chew.'

Greg let out a tired sigh.

'You and Chris have so much fun though, I just didn't want to be left out.'

I was consoled, comforted by this confused idea of joint responsibility.

He continued: 'We're like, good kids trying to be bad. We're not hustlers. We're not street kids. We're doing this for fun. It's just not fun anymore.'

'Well,' I said, reassuringly. 'I got your arse.'

He smiled weakly.

'And I like yours.'

I grinned and leaned in for a kiss.

I followed Chris into the hallway, reaching a door with a hanging stick figure of a man. I imagined him sitting slumped on the moist, checkered floor, eyes purple and red from being rubbed too many times and sniffling.

I looked at the door between us, helpless and worried, and for the first time, felt a longing to dive headfirst into the ocean, stand on the floor, and let the calm swim around us.

'Chris, it's Jax,' I said, knocking. 'They took Greg in to see the doctor. Did Eli tell you what time he was going to come get us? You can let me in now.'

The door opened and his light brown eyes sat out of their sockets, black bangs flat on his dark forehead. I threw my arms around him, clutched him to my chest tightly, and hoped he would feel peace of mind, knowing he had done his best to clean up after us, making sure we found a way home.

'You have really soft skin,' he mumbled.

I smiled.

'You know I was out the moment they hit me right?'

'Yeah.' My head started to throb. 'Greg's quite a hero, isn't he?'

'It's just 'cause he's a big guy.'

'But you made sure we'd be taken care of.'

The tinted windows in the single-stalled toilet opened up to the decaying urban landscape. The giant skyscrapers I saw right outside the stained glass box soothed my soul. Every time someone sneezes there's a new store. Soon, we'd be huffing the

101

exhaust, out on the bustling streets home.

'I mean it,' Chris said, breaking up my thoughts. 'I don't know any other girl who'd be so cool about all this.'

'I don't really have a choice. I was there too, y'know.'

His face was really close to mine. I could smell blood and alcohol.

I knew there was only one real way to cheer him up. I puckered my lips and fell face forward.

*

That night, we could've become some urban legend. But we were three kids who got served. Learned their lesson. Let's face it. Smitty, our so-called mate, ripped us off. He sent us a multitude of texts for months after, trying to cajole his way back into our circle. We ignored him. My parents asked why we weren't at his place anymore and I pretended not to hear them. Fa'a Yu didn't want the police led back to him, so he stopped answering our calls. I'd see him from time to time in class, but he'd leave before everyone else got out so I couldn't talk to him. Greg's parents didn't believe his rugby-fight story, and he had to take Chemistry summer school before his A-levels anyway, so we saw him less. We were ordinary kids who drugged themselves into nothingness to avoid the shame of doing nothing. Too scared to be outlaws, too lucky to not have to be. That night was a way out of it all, but it couldn't be all that simple. I guess if it had never happened, I would still be with my best mate Chris on one side, and my other best mate Greg on the other, hoping to pass for eighteen-year-olds.

# FIELD, BURNING
Ysabelle Cheung

I start at the bottom, as I do on most days: a servant to the slow and steady sweep. In the morning there are no crowds, only the yolk of the sun and a few whistling rock thrushes, disappearing into the gaping maw of the mountain. It's a Wednesday, early enough to catch the light salty breeze lifting from the harbour. I take lunging mouthfuls of air punctured with rain and foamy sea. Up here, way up here, I can see the flat tongue of land where the city lies at the base of the mountain. Every so often the distracted sound of drilling perforates the air: then, silence. In Hong Kong, buildings are being torn down, built up again in glass and steel, spilling onto cramped streets.

There are dozens like me, grave-sweepers, tiny black specks mushrooming on the hillside, dragging rusty oil drums and brooms and stretching our bony palms for a dollar or two. Blackened fingers. A dollar or two, to ease the pain of this life.

Each day I sweep and collect and pray. What else can I do? I am now eighty years old. I am terrified of the inner-city cacophony, teeming with Western riff-raff and too-skinny sexless people dressed like aliens. I am scared of the living. So I live by the dead, with my collection: blackened cans for burning paper money, rejected joss sticks picked up from funeral homes, dried white flowers hanging upside down from their stalks. I get by. I beg for money from grave visitors, and help them burn their papers and slice open the roasted-pig offering as they wipe away tears. 'Imagine if death did not exist,' I say to them brazenly, as only an old haggard Chinese auntie can. 'Life would not even matter, eh?'

They smile awkwardly, blinking through their tears, not

recognising the truth of my words.

I wait. I eat. I hobble. And every night before I sleep, I light eleven joss sticks and perform a humble ritual for the girls I let go, for the pain I caused, and to beg for forgiveness. *Please, please, let me die.* I smell burning flesh every time, a tangled, hot smoke that brings it all back: a caved-in face, a hand turned to black ash, the wet lick of a flame. This is my punishment. I take it willingly, but I am tired. I desperately want to die.

A Wednesday. A day like any other day, but my routine is disturbed. A man comes by with a funeral director to the plot of graves by my little shack and when he sees me loitering by the premises, calls me over.

'*Por por,*' he says, addressing me as his grandmother, out of respect. I notice his smooth, high forehead, underscored by eyes carved into his face like two wet stones. He is grieving. 'Good morning. Do you know which way the wind rises on this side of the mountain?'

I splutter, 'I don't know…'

The winds are not my concern.

'Can you tell us anything about this particular plot?' He points at a white square of land beneath him, textured with grit and rubble.

I shake my head, and explain, 'Sorry, I'm just a grave sweeper, I just live here…'

'You live in the cemetery?' he asks then. The funeral director, I see from the periphery of my vision, shakes his head. I hear him whisper: 'She's the mad lady on the hill—everyone knows about her.'

'It's quiet here,' I defend. Who was this man? And why did he ask so many questions? Infantile child, meddling with an old lady. I'm older than you know; I have lived a hundred years more than you have. I turn to go back into my house.

'Wait!' He calls out. '*Por por,* I'm confused. My wife's family asked for her to be buried here, but I don't know why. This plot is twice as expensive as others directly next to and behind it. I just want to know why this particular spot is so special. Do you really not know anything?'

I feel a twist in my solar plexus.

'Your wife?'

'Yes. She passed away last week.' He speaks softer now. 'Her name was An.'

I feel something drop out of the bottom of my stomach. My heart perhaps.

'Good evening,' I stammer and retreat into the spotty shadows of my house once more.

I hear him calling me again for a while but then he leaves with the funeral director, asking aloud again why the plot was so expensive.

I can't sleep that night. The man's stony sad eyes keep coming back to ask me, 'Who are you? What do you know? Why is this spot so special?'

Eventually I get up to drink a glass of water. It stews in my belly like acid. I look out of my tiny window and see the pregnant white moon and all the light that are the stars circling it. They are telling me everything and nothing. Signs are only what we make of them.

*She has to be buried there*, I think to myself. *This will fix it all. This is where the story will end, finally.*

I sit down heavily on the bed and draw out a sheaf of rice papers, in cereal colours. Money for the dead; it will have to do as writing paper. Slowly the words begin to take shape and my story, after so many years of being carried in my heart, is finally told.

Dear An's husband,

I am sorry. I did not even ask your name.

I can't be certain as to why An's family asked for her to buried in that particular plot, but I've lived in my little house for twenty years now and everyone knows me as the mad lady on the hill. Mad I may be, but here is what I know.

If An's family have heard of me and know that I'm here, maybe they remember that I was once their neighbour. One day when An was young, she was involved in a terrible car accident and I rescued her from under the vehicle.

To you, a stranger, I am begging—please buy that plot, and bury your dear wife there. I will explain it all in this letter, why this is important to me. If you are hesitant about reading on, I should probably tell you this now: I once had a daughter called An and the Chen family—your wife's descendants, I believe—are very familiar to me.

Another thing you should know is that I have been alive on this earth for over a hundred and fifty years. Do you believe in reincarnation?

I'm so very tired now, of this guilt, of this shame, of watching repeated acts of violence as a reminder of what I did.

But I do not excuse for it and I confess: I am a murderer.

And this is my story.

My name is Zhang Wen. I am a midwife. Correction: I was a midwife. But that was a long time ago. A lot can change in a century and a half.

Childbirth was painful back then. We had no drugs, only prayer. The herbs we used to alleviate ill symptoms of pregnancy were no match for the total liquidation of the female form, her genitalia and dark leaky corners and soul, as another creature was pushed out and out. In the midst of blood and excrement and fear and pain a tiny squashed thing would squirm its way out, a thing that takes a breath and cries—and begin in the world as a human being. My job was to make sure that journey from the mother's belly to the cruel world was a safe passage. I did this for thirty years, living in a small village in the Shandong province, wiping my fingers and forearms clean of the blood every night.

Now you could say I am a murderer.

Everything in this world, evil, pure, is plucked from a single thought in the human mind. The clothes on your back. The spoon in your mouth. Love. Books. Music. Death. I had not heeded the words of my mother, who knew of this, and the power of the moment when holding a naked screaming shiny babe up to the light. I became arrogant with this power, wanting to have that final roll of the die.

After what I did, my daughter threw herself into the lake out of shame and my husband left me. I hanged myself, but I couldn't die. I've been reincarnated fifty-three times. Every time I close my eyes I'm forced to open them again. I've seen the fickle truth of human nature; the cycle of violence that is swallowed and spat out, each time a new form and a new face. I lived as a pigeon, shot through with pellets and kicked around for fun by delinquent teenagers; I lived as a disembowelled sheep, burning alive on a pyre; I lived as a dumb fly, hopelessly magnetised to shit; I lived as an old bitch, watching and howling as a woman was knifed and raped to death on a resident street in New York, where dozens of other block occupants turned a blind eye and ear. And I kept living and living when all I want to do is die, or at least to forget. Well. I do not know if they are the same thing.

I am human again for the first time since the incident, and in Hong Kong, trying to piece together what this could mean and why I'm here. I think I know. This could finally be my last life. Because just across the road from where I used to live in Hong Kong, a little girl called An was born into a wealthy Eurasian family and, one December day, I saved her from a car crash. This was your wife.

After killing so many and watching so many die, how does it feel to save again? To give back life? I knew when I extracted the tiny broken-limbed An, a girl who looked so much like my own daughter, from the crash and breathed the life back into her, that this was my chance. She gazed up at me in a somnambulatory daze, barely conscious, and I thought I heard her murmuring, 'Save me, save us...'

My heart started pounding again after being dead for so long. I discovered that An's family were descendants of the eminent Chen clan from the Shandong region. My home region. My heart opened and bled with the possibility of sweet, silent death.

I saved An when I was only a teenager but still I wasn't dead yet. I was afraid that if I forced it—jumped a building or pressed the cool nozzle of the gun against my temple—I would start the process again and be born as something else. A cockroach. A measly worm. So I lived, but each night waited for death.

Every night I smell that burning flesh again.

There were eleven girls and I was midwife to all eleven, and dozens more in the village where I once lived with my husband, daughter, and mother, in the late 1800s. The province of

Shandong was soft with apricot and peach blossoms in the spring and blessed with gold bouncing hectares of corn and wheat in the fall. Our home was our clinic. The house had been in our family for generations, insufferably moist in the summers and sharp with frost in the winters, but age had also given it grand character. The walls were ecru patterned with damp weathering, but our *kangs* and rosewood chairs and tables slept under one roof in harmony. The kitchen was always steaming with various pots and boilers of herbs and roots and our living room doubled as the doctor's room, the medical table discreetly hidden by a silk folding screen. I usually delivered babies at the mothers' homes but everything else—anything from moxibustion to acupuncture—was performed within those four walls. It was a familiar life. I had grown up seeing my grandmother and mother bearing fine needles pricked with scarlet, been told at the dinner table how to tell the sex of a baby. If the stomach protrudes pointedly, a boy; if it is round and circular, a girl.

'Only women can be midwives,' my mother would always say to me. 'It is a special gift we have. And in our family, you are destined to be one too.'

I started my training when I was barely an adolescent, counting the fevered pulses of my cousins and sisters in imitation of medical consultation. This was how the girls in our family played doctor, and to me that was just what it was—play. I had no interest in babies or giving lungs to a half-living thing. I didn't know what any of it meant.

I delivered my first baby when I was fourteen years old. My mother was in the room supervising, grabbing my hands this way and that, scolding and pinching. The patient, a girl barely older than me, frightened me with her sad chicken bone hips. Her tiny frame seemed closer to snapping with every millimetre of dilation, her pale mottled thighs jerking wildly in protest. The whole thing was a dance, as she pulsed and pulsed and pulsed the thing out. The head crowned after five hours and the babe came out shockingly puckered, soaked in a scarlet, syrupy glaze.

We waited, my mother and I, for the baby to cry. The patient had already passed out from exhaustion. The light broke around us in the early morning like a cool daze. In that room painted with blood, the earth beneath my feet seemed to shake like jelly, but the baby never uttered a single sound.

It was then I started to understand that midwifery was not simply a delivery of life, but a way to save a baby from drowning in death, every time, and from that point on I felt an irresistible pull to save them. The grief of the blue baby—that was natural. What I didn't expect was the uncomfortable but seductive stirrings of something I later recognised as power.

I gave birth to my own little girl when I was nineteen years old. I watched, drowsy with prickly heat, as my mother held up An by the legs like a frog and patted her tiny buttocks. 'Good girl!' My daughter gave a sharp shriek and there it was: a new life. My husband and I spoiled her. We fed her cold plums that dribbled juice down her plump chin and wrapped her in silky goat's wool all the way from Mongolia.

An was a sweet child. Prone to breaking out in smiles, she only fussed when the house smoked up during an intense herb simmering session. Sometimes it would take days to melt four quarts of herbal soup into one thick black bowl. The acrid smell was enough to drive away any bug or mammal from the vicinity. An never got used to it. When she was younger she would vomit uncontrollably and later, she would alleviate her nausea by sitting in the courtyard and placing a tea-drenched cloth over her face.

Our family bucked convention but still commanded respect from neighbours because of our influence in the medical field. We did not bind An's feet or force her into midwifery, and she had, I believe, one of the most blissful childhoods of anyone in the province. I, not my husband, was the head of the family, in both power and income. But it all ended too early.

On her fifteenth birthday, my husband took An out to the fields to watch the sunrise while my mother and I saw patients. I was always shielding An from the operations within the clinic room; out of protectiveness, and yes, a little out of selfishness. My mother was a resilient and steadfast midwife, for sure, and the other women in my family too, but I had a special talent for saving babies. Only two had ever died in my care, compared to the dozens others had haunting them. An could choose any path she wanted, but in the clinic room, and in the province, my rule was absolute.

Two ectopic pregnancies and a mild fever later, An and my husband came back and separated into their bedrooms without a word, despite me calling them to help with dinner. I sought out my daughter first, but she was reticent and confused. My husband was no better.

'Some people have arrived,' was all he offered.

We didn't know who they were back then—to us, they were just the *guizi,* foreign devils—and at first we shared our meagre lives with them. Confucian ways had taught us to be generous and hospitable with neighbours, but they razed our plump corn to the ground, leaving barely anything for our children and families, and started bringing in large shipments of metal, forcing our men to work for them. They converted our temples into their own churches. Who were they to tell us what to do, where to lay our cows to sleep, how to slice up our wild lands into industrial spaghetti? We took the bitter pill lying down, believing they would be gone after the harvest season. But they never left.

'It will be all right,' my mother, always the sensible one right up until she lost her senses, would tell us. 'Don't get in their way.'

We ignored my mother, of course.

My husband joined the Plum Flower Boxing Army, a collective of wiry men young and old who believed the spirit soldiers would aid them in their mission for foreign cleansing. I couldn't help but curse unholy spells under my breath whenever a *guizi* walked by. My eyes flagged sin everywhere. Their raw milky stench was the devil's breath; their intrusion of the land was rape. Every natural disaster that befell Shandong from that point on was another sign from above. We starved. We struggled. And all the time the *guizi* were getting plumper, and all the time they were getting richer.

Even now I can't help but shake with fury, or at least with the memory of that fury.

I learned this Christian maxim when I was dying out my

fourth life as a mouse in an abandoned church. I slept and pissed in a chewed-out hole in a Bible and the words faced me every day. John 8:7: *Let he who is without sin cast the first stone.* Yes, they took our land, they took our crops, they even took the women. But even still, who was *I* to play God? Those words burned into me like a fire of shame. My sin was abusing my power and I cast that stone too far out. Why did I have to get involved?

One morning I walked past one of the new *guizi* buildings to collect worm root with An and came across a lady dressed in blue silk, leisurely fanning herself. She looked startled when I called her name.

'Chen Tai Tai,' I questioned, eyeing her swept-up hair. It revealed her long, swan-like neck where four plump beads of sweat trickled their way down. Her pearly fingers clutched an intricate gold-leaf fan which looked like something from the city, a gift perhaps. She was wealthy—from an aristocratic family—but I was used to seeing her in less flashy attire. Especially in the daytime.

'Oh…' she turned. 'Doctor Zhang. And hello, An.'

She seemed rattled by my presence. Odd, considering I had known her all her life. My own mother had birthed her, so she was like a sister to me, and I had cut the cords of three of her sons and seen her almost die over the fourth, whose tiny black lung had grown inwards in the belly. He wouldn't come out. She exhausted herself for days, bereft of breath, oozing a snaking, quivering sweat, trying to push, trying to live.

I knew Chen Tai Tai's husband, the leader of the Plum Boxing Army, had a temper. More than once she had turned up at my doorstep with a smashed bone here, or a damp dark bruise there, crying that she had failed as a woman and as a wife. It had been especially bad the weeks after she had lost her fourth son, and even I had not been able to escape punishment under this man's dark gaze. 'Save the boy,' he had said. 'Four boys. That's what I asked for. That's what I paid for.'

But instead I pumped her with herbs; I heated thick, pressed stumps of mugwort against her skin until I saw the blood rise in her cheeks again. The boy I could not save. Punishment came a week later when a burning bush appeared in my courtyard, but putting out those flames was a mild inconvenience compared to the state Chen Tai Tai was in when I went to visit her a few days later. This was a husband's way of delivering a message, and the boxing army leader's cautionary warning: *I won't forget this disobedience.*

Chen Tai Tai fanned herself silently, slowly now. My new eyes told me something: *sin.*

'I've been meaning to visit you, Doctor,' Chen Tai Tai said quietly, bowing her head. Her cheeks sat like freshly steamed dumplings on her face as she smiled, and I was reminded of how pretty she actually was. And then in her expression I saw something more. I noted her pulse, which throbbed from her neck, a slow, heavy pulse, and the milky sheen on her forehead. She wasn't showing at all, but the curves on her already voluptuous figure carried an extra pound or two. She was clearly with child.

'There are a few of us—girls—and we have a rather unusual request of you,' she continued.

But then a man stepped out of the building and Chen Tai Tai pressed her lips together. He did not walk down the path but stood next to her, and the guilty bitch looked down at the floor.

The *guizi* smiled and held out his hand—not to me, but to An, who trembled and stepped back.

'You should be ashamed of yourself,' I spat to Chen Tai Tai. 'An, let's go.'

I should have listened to my mother. *Don't get in their way.* Later that night, I fumed and thrashed in my bed, imagining Chen Tai Tai with her devil lover, cursing her stupidity but mostly directing my attention and energy towards the *guizi*. It tortured me that he was swimming in sweet flesh that belonged to *us,* that his rough hands were caressing the body that I had nursed back to health. They had infected us, our colony. I wished, wickedly, for his death, for her death, and for their skeletons to kneel at my feet in repentance.

I dreamed that Chen Tai Tai and her *guizi* man were trapped in a giant sac of amniotic fluid. I held a very thin, very sharp needle that could release them. I poked and the viscous liquid oozed out, the bodies of the traitors tumbling out naked and sweaty. *Thank you, thank you for giving us life*, they said, but then I smiled and then stabbed them over and over and over again with the very thin, very sharp needle, until they were both bloodied and dead.

Everything in this world, evil, pure, comes from a single thought, from the mind.

I wonder sometimes, now, who it was that tossed that pebble first. It's taken over a century and fifty-three reincarnations for me to face the reality that it could have been me. Because a week after I cursed that devil man and his whore, my little girl walked into a *guizi* church to beg for a bag of rice and crawled back out with blood on her dress.

It's difficult for me to trace back to the what and the why; everything happened so long ago, and these days I'm left with a drifting sense of loss rather than memories that I can pick up, hold, and scrutinise. The images of those I loved, those I knew, float in a glass bowl of water, and often I can't see clearly—my husband's face, An's smile, even my mother's voice, they're all pulled and melting in the liquid, distorted like oil. But I try to remember.

If a baby's cry is the purest sound in the world to me, the most terrible one is the sound of your child's soul dying.

My palms were sweaty before An even came back to the house—two spots right in the centre of my hands throbbed as if a thick needle had been jabbed through them. I felt nauseous, and thought, *that's not right*. Then I heard the door open, and thought, *that's not right at all*.

Then I saw An's face and was incapable of any further thought.

I must have fainted because I next remember lying on the *kang* with my mother standing over me, frowning as everything swam in an awful fog.

'You, stay there. I will look after An,' mother said sternly. From outside the room where we saw our patients, I heard mother's voice like birdsong, soothing, desperate: 'An. An. My darling granddaughter, my beautiful child.'

And then the occasional, softer cracking sound of my little

girl's heart breaking—so quiet that if you didn't know or listen, you wouldn't have heard. The examination took almost until dawn but, from then on, I did not get a good night's sleep ever again. At first I was distraught. I couldn't help thinking it was somehow my fault, that I hadn't protected An enough and that I had cursed the *guizi*. Karma has a way of clawing its way back. But slowly that depression ate its way into anger, an acidic, toxic fury that drove me half insane.

'Who was it? Which one of those dirty foreigners was it?' I'd shake my daughter, making her burst into hot soggy tears.

'She's young,' my mother said to me when she saw how I fussed and checked in on An every hour. 'She will survive this. We should keep her in the house for a few weeks—say she's taken a trip to the city to visit a relative. No one can know about this.'

The shame of women! But my mother was right, as always. My mother—always the sensible one, I thought. I should have noticed then that something in her had changed too. How could it not have? Irrationality of human nature blinds people at best, but at worst, lets the spiders into your brain to pull you this way and that.

My mother started screaming in the night first, gurgled cries that woke the cockerels in the yard. It took minutes, longer even, for me to jerk her awake. I'd shake her repeatedly until I saw the dead tiny black circles in her eyes come into focus again—they were always wide open.

'The gods are displeased,' was all she'd mutter when I'd finally force her awake. 'The sinners must repent.'

She began to wander out into the courtyards at night, and then the fields, too fast for us to chase her. She roamed the streets, sobbing, falling to her knees. And then one morning, she could not speak any more. We tried everything— acupuncture, stuffing herbs down her throat, grinding the soft fur of a hundred bees together to make a paste—but all in vain. In fact my mother seemed to enjoy our efforts in making her talk again; she developed a crooked smile that one might have called sly. She forgot about An, who was slowly turning into jelly, lying in bed all day. She forgot about us. She forgot about midwifery. One evening, my husband found her in a rice paddy field, dunking her head in the water over and over again. He had been practising with the Plum Flower Boxing Army, and they were halfway through their spirit-calling exercises when they heard her screeching right across the field.

The witch doctor was called in and pronounced my mother dead and gone. 'She's no longer your mother,' she said. 'What you have here is a bird fairy.'

'Bird fairy?' I shivered.

The witch doctor reassured me that bird fairies were harmless—in fact, they often had premonitory hindsight that could prove useful for harvest and protection from natural disasters. She suggested that we tie it up in the courtyard with the moulting, sick roosters, and at that awful humiliating proposal I broke and pleaded.

'There must be some other way,' I said, looking helplessly at my mother, who was slowly chewing at a burlap sack, fingers clenched like claws around the noose of the bag. 'She's still my mother.'

The witch doctor shook her head.

'Each human, creature, and insect on this earth has a soul,' she explained. 'Your mother's soul has departed and strangely, another has immediately taken its place. She is not simply possessed. She is gone.'

Where had my mother's soul gone then? That night, I dreamed of tiny leafcutter ants, all lined up on a hundred-year-old tree that was burning. Large drifts of charcoal smoke floated down from the branches like clouds. Every time an ant reached a certain point on the tree it burst aflame, but carried on walking. I had an odd feeling that every one of those ants carried a minuscule part of my mother's soul and they were trying to get up to the top of the tree to piece it all back together but kept dying on the way. The ants sounded like they were screaming as they died and I covered my ears, but then I realised that it was me that was screaming, and at that point, I woke up.

The moon was a pregnant sphere of white light. I got up to drink some water. On the way to the kitchen, I passed An's bedroom and saw her curled up in a foetal position at the bottom of her bed.

Carefully, I covered her frightened little body with a blanket and then continued on my way down the corridor. Passing one of the windows, I saw my mother—now the bird fairy—outside, tied up against a tree. Her eyes were closed and she was squatting, ass sticking out as if she had a plume of feathers skirting off her back.

In the kitchen, I poured myself a cup of cold water and drank it slowly.

I began to shake. It started like a tremor, then grew into a seizure, and soon the entire kitchen felt like an earthquake. I was the epicentre, the hate still inside of me.

The next morning, my husband found me lying on the floor, arms and legs akimbo in a pile of broken crockery. I had smashed every single last plate, cup, saucer, and dish in the kitchen.

'Something has to change,' he said as he helped me up. He said it in response to the look in my eyes, because he had felt that earthquake too.

They came a week later, calling: 'Please, Doctor Zhang. Doctor. Doctor.' Small flat coins falling from their palms. Eleven girls gathered outside in the courtyard with the moulting roosters, the bird fairy, and the sparse winter fern, which picked at the ground in frosty droops. Chen Tai Tai stood at the front accompanied by a handmaiden. Despite the fierce winds, she remained upright like a slender bamboo pole. The others were wives of farmers, millers, cotton-pickers, skin darkly wind-bitten like the red sorghum that sprang in the fields. I sat in the warmth of my midwife room, watching them shake in the sleet and airless Shandong wind. My front door remained locked as I debated whether to let them in.

It was clear that almost all of the eleven girls were suffering either from malnutrition (highly probable, considering the shortage of food), fever, or anaemia. I watched how they took to the wind, the temperature, to the heavy sky which seemed to glow a gaunt cilantro colour. It was not the season, year or even decade for pregnancy. I had checked the calendars and the forecast and the signs had told me so; but even without divine consultation I could plainly see from the weather and the lack of crops that these babies would all be born into desperate poverty.

The bird fairy was the only one who seemed to be having fun. She taunted the girls, sticking out her tongue and crowing manically, circling them. Every so often she would hop and look to the sky, seemingly wanting to take off, but never quite managing to leave the ground.

'Doctor Zhang!' Suddenly Chen Tai Tai's voice rang out. 'You must let us in!'

I unlocked the door.

'Only one,' I said, beckoning. 'Chen Tai Tai. You.'

I had questions, but when I saw that woman move into my corridor, I fell silent. The luminous glow which I had first seen a few weeks ago by the *guizi* building had now developed into something else; fine webs of pale blue covered her body in a withered map. Her veins were popping out. My gut instinct kicked in and I reluctantly set up the necessary equipment for a consultation. I gave Chen Tai Tai a spitting bowl and gestured for her to expel. She coughed—a wet, loud cough—and a bracket of phlegm plunked into the bowl. It was dotted with blood.

I checked her pulse, which now raced at rabbit speed, and checked her eyes, nose, ears, and mouth. Tuberculosis.

'How have you and your... husband planned for this child?' I asked, eyeing her reaction as she tugged at the corners of her mouth with a handkerchief.

'He doesn't know, doctor.'

'You do know that, with your illness, the baby would have a very low chance of survival, even in the womb. You have a personal herbalist in the Chen household, am I correct?'

'Correct.'

'And in his weekly medical examinations, he never spoke of your condition?'

A pause, then she smiled weakly: 'Doctor, if my herbalist had spoken to my husband about my condition then I wouldn't be coming to you. I wouldn't even be here.' There was a pause.

'We need safe passage to Hong Kong.' She said it in such a small, low voice that I almost thought I had imagined it.

'We?'

'The girls and I. We are going with the… we are boarding a ship on Saturday at sundown. We would like to ask if you would join us, and look after us. Of course, you will be handsomely rewarded. Your family can come too.'

Freedom: I saw it in Chen Tai Tai's eyes, and just for a brief moment I pictured her as a broken, bruised slip of a girl coming to my door in the dark of the night. Crying on my lap, wishing she was dead. I almost relented just then. Almost.

But I had one more question: 'Why have you not told your husband?'

She fell silent.

'It's—the baby—is not my husband's.'

I narrowed my eyes.

'The baby's father, my lover. He is a *guizi*.'

There it was. The confession. It all swirled in my head like a dark liquid, the violation of my pure daughter, the *guizi* devastating our land, Chen Tai Tai spreading herself before the dirty foreigners, like a bitch in heat. Ah, so this was who she was escaping with.

'Get out.'

'Doctor, please—'

'Leave now or I will alert Master Chen to your condition.'

She lunged from her chair. Her forehead glistened with fever.

'Doctor, I hope you will not mind me being so forward. But as a woman to another woman—I think you should know—we will not stop coming. You are a doctor, and you are supposed to cure us, save our babies. We have come to you because you are the only safe refuge left, whether we like your company or not. Because you will not see us and come with us, I have to say this on behalf of the other ten girls out there: our choices are ours to make, as are yours.'

She left with the other girls, steps never faltering, even when the bird fairy clawed the hem of her skirt. I watched from my window; my eyes did not deceive me now. Eleven sweet, soft, swollen bellies, all carrying *guizi* foetuses, the blood from the rapists of our land and of my daughter. Escaping their sins by boat with the devils.

That night I brewed my cup of dark rage over supper. Anger, like power, is an addictive blood to feel in your veins, and back then I had both coursing through me: a sick potion.

I knew there were other people who felt the same. The Plum Boxing Army men. Dozens of them, lined up, ready to kill. Some no older than An, others boasting swathes of grey round the temples like my father. Each in body like a tree, plump thighs like those of a trunk, arms battling the wind like branches. Their faces a punched violet like fat plums as they look to the sky to summon the spirit soldiers.

Some thought they were crazy, relying on divine powers rushing down from the heavens to save the day, but everything seemed crazy at the moment. If we couldn't rely on faith, what else?

'I'm coming with you to practise tomorrow,' I said suddenly to my husband, while lying in bed later on. He rose on his elbows and looked at me, my husband of so many years.

'Are you sure?' was all he said. I could have turned back then. I was granted another night of reflection, to consider my actions and to take a step back from the situation, but I was too deep in it. I was furious and I wanted to show the *guizi*, and yes, those girls too, that just as I could give life, I could take life. I wanted to avenge my daughter. I wanted to take back Shandong.

That morning when my husband and I reached the edge of the field just past five thirty, I knew exactly what I wanted to say.

The Plum Boxing Army General walked in long strides, across to where we were standing, and saluted both of us. Chen Tai Tai's husband was tall and wiry but commanded authority best with his eyes, which were so deep and black that they seemed like water pools. I knew he was not a gentle man. I *knew* this. Yet I continued with my mission and my task and tried to convince myself that because it was his wife, because they must have shared love once, he would be kinder. I pushed away the image, again, of Chen Tai Tai's milky complexion broken in by blooming dark spots.

He waited, silent.

'There's something you should know,' I began, and from that point on, everyone's fate was sealed, including mine.

The day after that, it happened.

We were in the courtyard: me, An, and the bird fairy. I was urging An to practise her calisthenics, afraid that soon she would not be able to walk. Ever since the incident, she had been staying in bed all day.

'Huo! Huo!' the bird fairy screeched. Today she had decided that she could fly. Before breakfast we had to retrieve her from the roofs, where she had been circling the cramped expanse, about to leap. 'First came the fire, then the wind, then the water...'. She danced in her imaginary courtroom of fairies and deities.

'Tighten your pelvic floor muscles,' I was instructing An. I had allowed her to grow weak and her apple-white arms wobbled as if boneless. She planted her hands on her knees and squatted, lowering herself further and further. Then she stopped.

'Mother...'

I looked up. A thin, flagging ribbon of smoke. Joined by another, then another, then another, pluming to form a mushroom of ash. It was coming from the fields, where my husband was training already with the army.

'They must be performing a ritual to call upon the spirit soldiers.' I said.

'Huo! Huo!'

The General had promised that punishment would only be as severe as necessary. He had almost looked kind as he said this to me, and I noticed his pupils had changed colour, like black and indigo ink. I had expected flagellation at worst, forced abortions even. But when my husband did not come back home at the expected time of seven, as he did every night and had done for the past ten years, I felt my bones turn to ash with fear.

I made my own way to the fields. An odd, clustered sound echoed from far away, like a termite, scratching, scratching.

Walking further, I passed the *guizi* church again, the very one where An had lost her childhood. Outside, a man was smoking. He didn't move for the longest time, watching me as I walked briskly down the path. His face was reddened by the hot flump of the afternoon. I, too, watched him, from the corners of my narrowed eyes. The smoke from his cigar dissolved in tissues. He could have been the rapist, or Chen Tai Tai's lover, or both.

It was then that I realised: it didn't matter. It could have been any one of them, but knowing which one, slaughtering *that one*, wouldn't heal my daughter's wounds or change what had already happened. I was so, so arrogant. Of course I can't change the future or the past.

As if shaken from a dream, he snapped his back straight and headed inside.

The fields were black. As I approached them, it all looked like a mirage in the bright sun: the pockets of air suspended in smoke, the crimped grass, the Yellow River, spotted with black. And there it was, that sound, that scratching termite sound… it was the aftermath of the fire, that crackling pop of burnt skin lifting from burnt flesh. The faces were indistinguishable.

Something pulsed, moving, in the mass. It was a rat, drenched in water, its fur spiking. It ran over the women, sniffing their bodies, their bellies, the ashes of their singed hair, then over my feet, over towards the Yellow River.

They had set them on fire. Burned them alive, all eleven of the women, including the beautiful Chen Tai Tai, who would leave three little boys motherless.

I heard Chen Tai Tai's voice once more: 'We will not stop coming. You are a doctor, and you are supposed to cure us, save our babies.'

The edges of the field were marked by a moat of water where the men had thrown buckets over the fire. I had never smelled a burnt body before, let alone so many. At a loss, I roamed the fields, eyes itching, my shoes clinging to the black dirt. I encountered eyes, the gleam of a white tooth, a hairpin lost in the myriad of things. Later I found out that they had been ordered to strip naked before the army, flesh to air as if to reveal the very human sin they had committed. One last time, before the flaming torch struck. What would the fire fly to first? Their long bundles of hair, like silk, so carefully looked after? Their arching necks, oiled with the perfume of steamed flowers? Or their wombs, hiding the foreign devils in their sleep—would the fire have seen a likeness in its destructive evil? Burning. It was a terrible death, one that those eleven women didn't deserve. It was murder. Instead of saving them and their babies, I had driven them to the ground.

From that day on, I lived, and still live, with death in my heart and guilt in my soul. My daughter An went to the lake one morning and drowned herself. My husband vanished, taking with him any semblance of a family life we once had, and the bird fairy I released into the wild after she clawed my face one night.

Outside the walls of my house, I saw only more fire as the days rolled on. The Plum Boxing Army torched churches and the hot mist of blood birthed a diseased sunrise every morning. We, the victims, had become the enemy: *guizi* after *guizi* was slaughtered until their names did not matter anymore. This one, that one, kill, kill, kill. The madness of power that I recognised in myself ran like a river through Shandong, and then through China. Was this what I had wanted?

Not long after, I decided to hang myself.

It's a strange feeling, the moment before you actually take your own life. There's the debating, and the tears, and the cold membrane of numbness that wraps itself around your core. As the minutes tick by, you start to count *away* from life and towards death. Instead of *I am fifty-three years old, six months, two days, fifty-five minutes and thirteen seconds old*, you start thinking: five more minutes. Two minutes. Until the numbers diminish and it's like you're being reborn again in younger and younger seconds.

Here's how it went: the rope burned against my neck and I felt my throat convulse repeatedly, each time swallowing tinier and tinier parcels of air, until…

You know how this story goes from that point forward. Those history books you read as a boy? Narrative is kind to truth. Imagine being me, pulsing from life to life, helpless to save so many. The Boxer Uprising, the march of the Red Army, the rape of Nanking, the Cultural Revolution—our people fought for so much. We are resilient creatures. But the China I see now doesn't show the years of civilian struggle. Now, we are on the brink of another change, and the world is afraid of our power, but we will never once again be the land where sorghum grows for only our people.

My kinship sister, Chen Tai Tai, is the ancestor of your late wife An. Do you see now? You are the first person I have told my story to, dear, unfortunate stranger. But not a stranger after all, for you and I and everyone else in this world is tied to one another, whether we like it or not. I and you, you and An, An and Chen Tai Tai, Chen Tai Tai and I. An is destined to be buried next to my heart, as we wish for all our loved ones to be. She is Chen Tai Tai. She is my daughter. She is... she is... you must... my hands are shaking, sorry, this rice paper is too thin, my calligraphy is terrible... I *must* make you understand.

It is all so clear to me. I killed Chen Tai Tai and my daughter and pulled your wife back to life. I was destined to be born in Hong Kong, as human again, to do this. Now the soul I saved must come back to me and save me; the grave plot is waiting, and my death is too. I am the mad lady on the hill. I am mad. But wouldn't you be too, if you had lived one hundred fifty years knowing what you had done?

Please, please, bury An next to me.

Sometimes I think back to the time before it all happened, before the *guizi* came, before the violence, before the bird fairy. I look back to An's childhood, her young and strong little body dancing in the bedroom, my mother struggling to braid her thick black hair. Laughter, and the reassurance that yes, this life is important, because you only have one. In between the chapters of long, everlasting death and non-existence, life is short. In this memory the landscape has been restored to glory, and the trees are all in bloom. I hear the lilting whine of the sows in the courtyard pen. It is quiet. All is quiet. No one knows, or fears the future.

The purest sound in the world to me used to be the first breath of a baby. The quiet pulse of its heartbeat saying to me:

*I'm here, I'm here, I'm here.*

Now the only sound I wish to hear is nothing. Only in silence can I be free.

Sincerely,
Wen.

# NEVILLE'S PAINTING
Jason Y. Ng

The familiar clacks on the hardwood floor echoed through the elevator bank into the marbled foyer. Neville Hermann, a rotund forty-two-year-old law firm partner, swaggered down the hall and waltzed into his office at 10.15am. He had his leather briefcase in one hand and takeout breakfast in the other: congee with shredded pork and *yau tsah gwai*, a kind of fried dough that always left a grease mark on his mahogany desk.

While waiting for the congee to cool and his computer to boot up, Neville made a list of things he needed to do—or get his secretary Tracy to do—for the day. Pick up dry-cleaning. Confirm Friday lunch with Gemini Capital at the Hong Kong Club (they served the best suckling pig in town). Chase Dr Wong for test results. Neville had his physical exam last month and the results were supposed to come back from the lab last week. It was Monday and the clinic still hadn't called. This city was full of incompetent people, he thought. If only they were as good with deadlines as they were with their food.

His reverie was interrupted by the little red light on his Blackberry that blinked whenever a new email arrived. The message was from Gemini: *Sorry, Fri lunch no good. Same time Mon OK?*

He wondered what he would do with his suddenly free Friday lunch slot. Perhaps he would try that new Sichuan restaurant in Sheung Wan. He needed a reservation.

'Tracy!' Neville hollered, as if to a faraway butler in a twenty-bedroom estate. He was the Queen of England if she were into fried dough and suckling pig.

A feeble knock.

'Yes.' Tracy announced her arrival, clutching a notepad like a frightened animal.

'Could you move the Hong Kong Club reservation to Monday next week and see if that new Sichuan place has a table available this Friday? Do it before lunch, will you? And why is my office still so goddamn hot?'

'Oh, I already called them several—'

'What's name of the guy you talked to? What's his number?'

'Stan… Stanley from Facilities, extension 114. But he already told me—'

Neville interrupted his secretary again, this time with a heavy, bear-like growl, a growl that said *why must I do everything myself?* He dialled the extension and started to bark into the handset with unprovoked aggression.

'Stanley, this is Neville Hermann. It's a sauna in here. How many times does a partner need to call before you people get the temperature right? It's not rocket science, Stan.'

A pause.

'Don't make me call again.'

Click.

By now Neville had sucked up so much oxygen in the room that Tracy began to hyperventilate.

'You need to raise your voice to get things done around here,' he lectured his secretary as he shoved the finished takeout into the trash can, before rubbing his greasy fingers on the side of his desk. 'I haven't spent seven years living in Hong Kong without learning a thing or two about how you people work.'

*

Neville lived a good life, a comfortable life. With a generous housing allowance from the firm, he got himself in a three-bedroom apartment in Repulse Bay. He had a live-in maid who made a mean cheeseburger and restaurant quality pork chops. He spent his spare time playing poker in Macau and golfing in Shenzhen, although he hadn't touched his clubs for several months because of a lower-back pain. He also loved collecting things—from vintage wine to oil paintings and old maps—and spent most of his day in the office in front of the computer checking wine prices online. Considering that his father had spent his entire life toiling at an auto plant in the Detroit suburbs, Neville had done well for himself. Though he did not have many friends—a fact he attributed to his busy schedule—he was satisfied with the way his life in Hong Kong had turned out.

Neville was new to the local art scene and his collection was modest. What he did have he loved and talked about every chance he got. Last month at an auction at a Hollywood Road gallery, he bought a contemporary figurative painting by an up-and-coming mainland Chinese artist. The purchase was part investment and part bragging right, for he had outbid all the wealthy suitors, some of whom he recognised from *The Hong Kong Tatler*. The painting, his trophy of war, now hung proudly in his office and he looked at it many times a day with deep satisfaction. While he had paid more for it than he would have liked, the title of 'art collector' it conferred upon him was worth every dollar.

But something about the painting bothered him. It wasn't so much the subject matter—an old Chinese peasant weighing a common hog on a scale, typical of the postmodern realism coming out of China these days—as it was the frame itself. No matter how many times Neville adjusted it, the painting looked lopsided on the wall. That drove him mad because a painting that cost that much deserved to be hung straight. More importantly, he liked things to be in a certain way. Every object in his office was tightly controlled: the pencils were sharpened and aligned, papers were neatly stacked, and the two guest chairs faced a certain direction at all times. Everything, except for that stubborn painting. Each time he looked at it he would move it a little bit. One time he jiggled it so hard the nail fell out and the whole thing fell on the floor. Tracy rushed in to find out what happened and later called Stanley to put a new nail in the wall. After that the painting stayed level for a few moments, before it slid back to a crooked position.

\*

At noon, Neville took a taxi to his favourite dim sum parlour in Causeway Bay. It was a weekly expedition for him. Ever since the restaurant earned a Michelin star last month, there had been at least a twenty-minute wait for a table. That day he offered the restaurant manager fifty dollars to skip the line. The manager gave him a nervous laugh and said he did not wish to get into trouble. So Neville took a number and waited by the entrance like a grumpy school boy. Standing there on the sidewalk in the winter chills, he felt powerless. There were no secretaries to bark orders at and no junior lawyers to do his work. He was no better than the old hag standing in front of him, whose cheap sweater smelled like mothballs. Here in Causeway Bay, only three subway stops from his corner office in Central, he was just like everyone else.

With the shrimp dumplings and fried rice still gurgling in his stomach, Neville waltzed back to the office at 2.45pm. That's when Tracy delivered the bad news: she called the Hong Kong Club and there was nothing available until Wednesday next week.

'Did you tell them the reservation was for *me*?' Neville asked without looking at her.

She whimpered an answer.

'Tracy, I *specifically* asked you to call them this morning. For God's sake, how many times have I told you that this place gets booked up fast?'

Before Tracy could mount a defence, Neville was already on the phone with the restaurant. He proceeded to bully the manager into giving him a table for two for the following Monday.

Neville derived certain satisfaction from being able to get his way all the time.

'That's what's great about Asia, isn't it?' he said to himself after dismissing Tracy, all the while trying to make out if the painting facing him was still lopsided. 'You get away with all kinds of bullshit. Imagine trying to pull that off back home in Detroit, ha!'

These thoughts continued as the old peasant stared at him. The bronze scale on which the hog perched gave off a life-like shimmer. To his annoyance, the painting was as crooked as the first day he had had it hung.

'Didn't what's-her-face get booted off the plane for yelling at the flight attendant?' The name of the Hollywood diva escaped him. All he knew was that he would never move back to the US, for here in Hong Kong he had grown rather used to behaving like a diva himself.

Restaurant crisis averted, Neville spent the afternoon surfing the Internet looking for bargain wine. Though the law had become more a distraction than a job to him, he ran a successful practice. His client book was as thick as the fat around his waist. In the eat-what-you-kill world of corporate law, Neville brought in the kill and let his associates do the heavy lifting. His right-hand man was Matt Parker, a senior associate with all the fine qualities of a college football quarterback: quick, adaptive, and exceptionally benevolent. Matt had a way of disarming people and making them want to grab a beer with him on a Thursday night. Together, the two *gweilo* made a good team.

'Yo, can you pop by?' Neville summoned his quarterback on speakerphone. He had gone through Matt's first draft of the underwriting agreement and marked the daylight out of it with a red pen. He was ready to give his sidekick a real beating for turning in a piece of half-hearted garbage. Before doing that, he figured there was still time for his afternoon sugar rush. He had picked up a couple of doughnuts from a bakery in Causeway Bay after lunch. In a well practised move, he shoved one of them into his mouth and swallowed it whole like a python ingesting a baby pig.

A minute later, while the doughnut was mixing with the dim sum lunch in Neville's stomach, Matt showed up with a big smile, waving a bunch of computer printouts. He had started a fantasy football pool in the office and Neville came out on top after last night's game when the Cowboys beat the Redskins 28-23.

'You did good, chief. Check this out!' Matt said as he slid the scorecards across the desk. While Neville was checking his score and finishing the other doughnut, Matt picked up the document with red ink all over it and asked, 'Is this your markup of the UA, chief? I'll have it turned before Jakarta.' The quarterback grabbed his assignment and walked out of the lion's den unscathed.

\*

Early Wednesday afternoon, Neville and Matt headed out of the office for their business trip to Jakarta. As always, a Mercedes 500-series was waiting for them outside the office building to take them to the airport. In the car, Neville was annoyed with the driver for talking in Cantonese on the cell phone while he was trying to read an email on his Blackberry.

'Hey, turn off your goddamn phone!' He hit the back of the driver's seat in rapid succession.

'No, no, it was your secretary Tracy-ah. She make sure I have pick you up,' the driver defended in halting English.

'Well, I am here now, aren't I? So turn off that goddamn phone!' Neville yelled, before turning to Matt and saying, 'Don't you just love getting all colonial on these people?' He chuckled.

Matt didn't return the laugh. *Perhaps he didn't hear my joke,* Neville thought. *Perhaps I should repeat it.*

Neville prided himself on his wicked sense of humour. He considered himself the sort of company cut-up that everybody liked and teased. He was convinced that all those self-deprecating jokes about his baldness and his weight had made him a rather popular member of the firm. The thought of being both witty *and* popular put a smile on his face.

There were long queues at the airport security checkpoints. Chinese New Year was just around the corner and the city was preparing itself for the busiest travel period of the year. Neville was getting agitated, even though their flight was not scheduled to take off for another ninety minutes. He began mumbling to himself and looking at his watch frequently and emphatically. Twice he asked the security officers to open more lanes but his requests were ignored. He flapped his arms and stomped his feet, like a kid who had dropped his ice-cream on the floor. Heightened airport security in the post-9/11 world had turned air travel into a leveller of mankind: the same lines and tedious procedures for all.

*The airport ought to set up a separate fast track for VIPs and people willing to pay more,* Neville thought. *No, not just the airport, but also dim sum parlours and doctor's offices. Speaking of doctor's offices, why hasn't the clinic called?*

*

Two days later on Friday, the duo returned to the office. Neville would normally be in a good mood when a business trip finished at the end of the work week, for all he would do that day was go through the stack of mail on his desk. Not this time. Thirty seconds after he walked into his office, he started to scream.

'Tracy!'

'Yes?'

'Did Dan Brennan call while I was away?'

'Yes, Mr Brennan phoned Wednesday afternoon while you and Matt were on the plane. I left a voicemail on your cell phone. Did you not get it?'

'I *always* turn off my cell phone when I travel! I've been expecting this guy for a month and he's in town from London for only two days. Now why the hell did you not send me an email?'

Neville was livid. His heart was racing and his face was as red as the strawberry pudding he had taken from the plane and planned on eating before Tracy ruined his Friday. After all this time she had learned nothing, he thought. She was as useless as she was the first day she arrived at the firm.

'Can't you people do anything right?' He hissed as he slammed the door.

Before heading to the Sichuan restaurant for a late lunch, Neville drafted a strongly worded email to the head of HR. The subject line read *Re: Tracy Lo's Consistent Underperformance*. He was certain that it was the only way she would learn.

*

It was the start of another work week. There was an unmistakable whiff of Monday-morning malady in the office. As scheduled, Neville met up with the Gemini Capital managing director David Winfrey at the Hong Kong Club. Over the years David had given him a substantial amount of work and his legal bills had just reached eight figures.

Neville ordered a half-dozen signature Shanghainese dishes and a large pitcher of Tsingtao beer. The two talked about the upcoming IPOs and traded thoughts on the debt crisis in Europe. By the time desserts arrived—a Chinese-style petit four consisting of egg tarts, sticky rice cakes, and two types of flaky pastry puffs—the business talk had wound down and segued to lighter subjects.

'So do you still play golf with Jonathan?' Neville asked, fishing for an invitation to the next golf day. Jonathan Loehmann was a common friend they had met at the Rugby Sevens several years ago.

'No, not really, no,' David replied with a surprised look. 'You haven't heard, have you?'

Neville shook his head, ready for some juicy gossip. An extramarital affair gone awry, perhaps.

'Jon was diagnosed with stomach cancer last fall and he moved back to San Francisco for his chemo. Poor fellow, he's only forty-two. And he has a wife and two young kids.'

*The guy is my age!* Cold sweat streamed down Neville's back. He wondered if David was even talking about the same person. The Jonathan he knew was a marathon runner. He never smoked and barely drank. Neville, on the other hand, had been eating the same greasy, sugary, salty, MSG-laden food for as long as he could remember. He hadn't been to the gym in five years.

He suddenly remembered Dr Wong and the test results. *Why hasn't the clinic called?* Neville spent the rest of the meal listening to David moan about his wife, who wanted to move back to Boston. Neville wished his client would shut up and give him some peace. When the lunch bill finally came, it was accompanied by two fortune cookies. Neville instinctively snatched one of them and cracked it open. The fortune said: *Plan for the best, prepare for the worst.*

\*

After lunch Neville decided to walk back to the office. He would normally flag down a taxi to avoid the fifteen-minute walk. Not today. He needed the exercise and the time to himself. In the office, his swagger became a lumber. Sitting at his desk, he saw the old peasant in the painting staring back at him with a ferocity he had never noticed before.

Later that afternoon, Tracy came by with his mail along with a nicely wrapped box of chocolates. It was from a wine shop he had patronised heavily this past year, one of the many free gifts he would receive in the lead-up to Chinese New Year. Normally he would rip the box open immediately and chow down half the contents in a single sitting. In an unprecedented show of restraint, he decided to leave the chocolates alone. He called Dr Wong instead.

The earliest appointment available was after lunch, and only because there was a last-minute cancellation. The receptionist told Neville he should feel lucky for what he was given. At Dr Wong's office, even a high-powered law firm partner was no match for that cheap pleather-bound appointment planner. For the rest of the day Neville did nothing. He didn't feel like having his afternoon sugar rush. He didn't care whether Matt had finished the underwriting agreement or if Tracy had remembered to pick up his dry-cleaning. He had only one thought: *Why do bad things happen to good people?*

\*

The following morning Neville woke up at 6.00. He poured his own cereal instead of waking up his maid. On his way to the office, he gave a homeless man a fifty-dollar bill, the same bill he had offered the restaurant manager in Causeway Bay the week before. He even held the elevator for a delivery guy instead of pressing the 'close door' button on him like he normally would.

He arrived at the office at 8.15, the earliest in years. Tracy wasn't even at her desk yet. He still found his office unbearably hot but he decided to take off his jacket and leave Stanley alone. Neville then grabbed the box of chocolates the wine shop had sent him and placed it on Tracy's keyboard. He scribbled 'Thank you for all your help!' on a yellow sticky and stuck it on her computer screen. Next, he found the draft complaint email to HR and hit the 'Delete' button.

Across from his desk, the oil painting of the Chinese peasant weighing the hog glistened in the morning sunlight. Just hours before Dr Wong would hand down the final verdict, Neville Hermann felt good about himself, but the painting was as lopsided as ever.

# THE QUEEN OF STATUE SQUARE
Nury Vittachi

On the evening of the night she would change the world forever, Grace Inday Masipag was carrying a dirty diaper in one hand and a plastic bag of warm dog poo in the other. She threw both into the bin and washed her hands. And washed her hands. And washed her hands.

From the kitchen, she could hear the stilted conversation in the dining room.

'You're talking mai tai or Moutai?'

'What's the difference?'

'One's a cocktail; the other's a traditional Chinese liquor favoured by *tongzhi* for the past, I don't know, ninety years.'

'I guess on this patriotic occasion we should go for the comrades' one.'

'It tastes like alcoholic soy sauce.'

'On the other hand—'

'I suggest a bottle of Brandlin, Cabernet Sauvignon. It'll go well with the sole.'

'Fish?'

'Red wine is great with fish, if it's the right wine and the right fish.'

*Ikaw gago*, thought Grace, shaking her head internally. *Don't you know that you should never serve a rich Cab with a flaky white fish? It'll make the seafood taste sour.*

The domestic helper never drank alcohol, but her first employer had been a wine bore whose idea of conversation was to repeat his standard lecture to every victim cursed to endure a meal with him. She'd heard it so often she could deliver it herself.

'Cabernet's always good.'

'Get the Brandlin,' Samuel Cheuk said to his domestic helper, who had sensed that she was about to be needed and had materialised in the corner of her employer's eye.

Grace moved to the wine cabinet displayed prominently at the side of the dining room while the cook and the waitress placed several dishes on the table. '*Sik faan*,' said Cheuk ritually, as the diners noisily took their places. '*Hay fai-la*.'

As they helped themselves, the conversation drifted back to the main topic of the day, the week, the month, the year, the decade: Handover 2. Although these days, the newsmedia had stopped calling it that. Now it was the 'resumption' or 'absorption' or 'merger' or 'completion' or 'takeover', depending on your point of view.

In less than six hours, Hong Kong was due to become entirely integrated with mainland China. Samuel Cheuk, the Hong Kong government's fourth most-senior lawyer, was having an early dinner with a few close friends among the ten separate appointments he had that day. He'd had to schedule a home stop into his schedule so that he could get out of his day wear and into his formal evening wear for the midnight ceremony. Being fourth from the top was tough. The city's top lawyer was the figurehead, at least in name. But any actual work which accrued to the figurehead fell to the second-topmost lawyer. The third in line was responsible in name for getting any actual legal work done. But the fourth actually did the work. So it had all been down to Samuel Cheuk and his team.

Grace had been told to make sure that a simple Western dinner would be on the table by six so that Cheuk could leave by 7.15, to go escort semi-important dignitaries—i.e., businessmen—around, while his seniors went to the VVIP events. In the event, her boss and his friends had arrived at 6.39. The cook, a Chinese-Canadian named Wu, had guessed everything would run late and had timed the meal perfectly.

At the table, British Q.C. Edward Roop was holding forth on his favourite theme, as occasions to do so would soon dwindle to nothing. 'They're still talking about China *resuming* control of *Xianggang*, but that of course is rubbish. When we got here, Hong Kong didn't exist. It was wilderness, a fishing village—the *total* population was less than that of a single modern Hong Kong housing block.'

Cheuk responded with good-natured fake scorn. '*Aiyeeah*! For fifty years you've been telling the same story. Look at the numbers. How can you take credit for this miracle? It was the miracle of the ninety percent, not the ten percent.'

Hong Kong Indian judge Rajiv Sandarahlingam, whose dark skin spectacularly set off his prematurely white hair, raised one index finger. 'May I remind you, the workers were Chinese, the governors were English, but the people who actually created the things Hong Kong is famous for were Indian. The import-export industry was dominated by Indians. HSBC, Hong Kong University, Star Ferry—all started by Indians. Think of the words associated with this part of the world: shroff, coolie, congee, pagoda—all Indian words. Our community has always been the secret powerhouse behind this place.'

'Again, I go back to the numbers,' Cheuk said. 'How many of you are there? One percent?'

'Dates are numbers,' the Indian said. 'How long has your family been here? You came in the 1960s from Guangdong, like the majority of Hong Kong *yan*. My family has been here since the beginning. *Before* the beginning. That's *one century* before you were here. So who is the real Hongkonger?'

All three were doing too well out of Hong Kong to have any real dispute, so the debate continued like an elegant game of three-way ping-pong.

Grace Masipag, topping up the guests' wine glasses, let her mind drift. Outside she saw the sunset, more vivid than usual, a yellow-pink sky somehow throbbing. A song drifted from the block opposite, a tender Cantopop crooner. The rich, acid smells of food and wine filled the room. This evening she felt the flow of time thundering past like the Yangtze, yet individual seconds passed slowly.

Her employer took a sip of the Cabernet Sauvignon and then a mouthful of the sea bass. 'This fish tastes sour,' he said, turning to glare at her. 'That idiot chef always over-seasons everything.'

Exactly twenty-one minutes later, Cheuk threw down his napkin. '*Aiyeeah*, look at the time. Get Sonny.'

On the phone, she told the driver to hover outside the building, so that Mr Cheuk and his friends wouldn't have to lengthen their journey ten seconds by going to the basement car park.

The moment the door clicked shut behind the men, she turned to march down the corridor to the children's room, where Marcus and Sophia were transfixed by a cartoon on their holodeck. 'Bedtime,' she said.

'Aww,' they responded in perfect stereo. '*Wait.*'

'Bedtime,' she repeated, with a careful mixture of sternness and warmth. 'But first your bath. You can use that new bath-toy again. The one with the bubbles.'

She knew the power of ritual and the draw of active play. The kids raced to the bathroom. 'Me fuss,' said Sophia, the toddler. 'Me fuss.'

The tension sweeping the city was curious, Grace mused: this particular handover was proving more of an emotional wrench than the previous one, fifty years earlier, according to the greybeards interviewed on the ubiquitous media screens.

Grace had done a first degree in international affairs and a second one in computer science, both at universities in the southern Philippines. Then she found herself drawn to work for the church, but decided that the best way to prepare herself for that was to work as a domestic helper in Hong Kong. That way she could earn money during her working hours while getting experience by ministering to fellow workers during her time off. During her first degree she had written a paper on Manila-Hong Kong relations. The previous Handover, in 1997, had been a major geopolitical event—the delivery of a city from a fading world power to a rising one; from one ethnic group to another; from West to East; from past to future; from one distinct culture to a very different one. But the whole thing had run surprisingly smoothly. The agreement said that Hong Kong's legal and economic systems would remain separate for a further fifty years: it was a key plank of the 'autonomy' plan that had enabled the transfer of sovereignty to work without raising panic.

This meant that it was 2047 when Hong Kong would really become part of China. Both sides were of the same race and culture, so that handover should have been far easier. But many people felt a degree of discomfort. Hong Kong had always thought of itself as special: from now on, it was going to be just another city in China—and not even a particularly big or unusual one. Even in its own neighbourhood, it would be outshone by Guangzhou and Shenzhen, both of which were considerably larger, in terms of both geographical spread and population size.

Also, the change in legal systems worried many. China had become much more of a modern capitalist society than it had been in 1997, especially since the mini-crash of 2019 and the major crash of 2023. But it was still China: big, sprawling, and almost ungovernable. Corruption cases regularly reared their ugly heads, and the legal system didn't work the same way as Hong Kong's Western-style one. In China, if you were arrested, you were assumed to be guilty. The job of the judiciary was simply to confirm that the police had got the right people, and devise a punishment. It wasn't a bad system, as it transferred the fundamental analysis of the case to the people who were closest to it, the police who investigated the crime and made the arrests. Westerners had never understood the system, but Grace did. It resembled the way justice was meted out in the coastal village where she had grown up, one of the few Christian communities in Muslim Davao.

Yet the main fear factor was probably something less tangible, the feeling that Hong Kong was a delicately balanced house of cards, built to enormous height over a period of two hundred years, which was about to undergo an earthquake. That was the feeling sending people rushing to the airport.

As Grace considered the families she worked for, with their Western tastes, their use of English as their main tongue, and their culturally eclectic meals, she realised that Hong Kong was and probably always had been much more Western than people thought. People would see notes in guidebooks saying that the city was ethnically more than ninety percent Chinese and assume that the English-speaking expatriate community was negligible in number and influence. But that had never been the case.

Many of the people listed as Chinese had lived abroad or been born abroad. They had the personalities and habits of Canadians, or Australians, or British, or Americans. The majority of schools in Hong Kong still taught in English, as had been the case in living memory. All universities taught in English, and most of the larger businesses, from trading companies to retail stores, operated in English. For more than half its existence, the number of Hong Kong people who were expatriates, in the sense of residents who were born outside the city, numbered more than fifty percent of the total population. Hong Kong had always been more of an international place than a Chinese one.

She felt a vibration in her pocket, and stepped back into the doorway of the bathroom, where she was out of earshot but could still see the children. 'Yes? *Bakit?*'

A tiny, hidden, flesh-coloured receiver in her right ear delivered audio, and her responses were picked up by a microphone-antenna that was no bigger than a short, stray hair. Miniature bluetooth equipment kept people in mundane jobs sane.

Arunalatha's voice was panicked. 'Menuka's been taken.'

'What? What do you mean? What happened?'

'Keerthi was told to take her to the Tsing house. But they were separated there, and he doesn't know what happened to Menuka. Someone took her somewhere. I think to that man Ric. You know—'. Arunalatha was unable to speak further.

'Don't worry,' said Grace. 'I'll make some calls. We'll find her—we'll send someone. Call me back in fifteen minutes.'

Her heart was instantly thumping. Any incident involving a woman being sent anywhere near Ric Fu Da Xin was seriously bad news. But first things first. This is how it had to be. They all had a lot to do tonight. Forcing a smile on to her face, she approached the children. 'Time to hop out of the bath,' she said.

'Awww,' chorused the children.

'And I'll tell you a story in bed,' she added, lifting Marcus, then Sophia, out of the water and reaching for the talcum powder.

Exactly eleven minutes later, the children were in bed *and* asleep. Grace knew there was a certain type of bedtime story—full of magical, surreal imagery, told in whispers in the dark—that caused children to float away to dreamland at high speed.

By the time Arunalatha called back, the domestic helper had made several calls. 'Missy So's going to Statue Square,' Grace told her. 'She's going to see the Queen. They'll sort it out. It'll be fine.'

There was silence in response, although Grace knew that Arunalatha was listening. The poor woman must be in a state of utter terror. Eventually a whispered, cracked voice said, 'She'll be okay, won't she?'

'Yes,' said Grace. 'Menuka will be fine. I promise you. The Queen's on it. You just get on with what you have to do. We have to clean house tonight, all of us.'

After finishing the call, the helper felt her shoulders slump. Everything they had worked for *for years* depended on things going smoothly tonight. All distractions were unwelcome—particularly one as scary as one of their number being snatched by Ric Fu Da Xin. Fu was called a 'princeling' by the news media, but the word was too nice for him. He was a sadistic, power-mad monster, proud of the fact that his English name Ric was said to stand for *rapist-in-chief*. Ric Fu Da Xin liked women. But he only liked women who didn't like him—women who were terrified, screaming and struggling to get away. People delivered into his hands were never the same again. He particularly liked abusing domestic helpers, whom he saw as even more powerless than his normal victims, and less likely to complain to the authorities.

Menuka, the girl who had apparently been snatched by Fu's staff, was the teenage daughter of one of Grace's best friends, a Sri Lankan helper who had worked in Hong Kong for more than twenty years. She refused to think about what the monster planned to do to the girl.

Grace closed her eyes and tried to pray. But her heart was thumping so hard that all she could do was send a verbal arrow heavenwards: *Help us, Lord. Tulongan mo ako, panginoon.*

*

Missy So Hoi-shun wrapped her cloak around her and doubled her speed from a fast walk to a steady jog. It was a warm evening but she felt the need to hide herself in her clothing, sensing danger from all sides.

The young Hong Kong woman was on a mission. She had always been a political animal, driven by a desire for social justice, and tonight was the culmination of her efforts. Over the past few decades, the political life of the city had stagnated, with power concentrated in the hands of wealthy special-interest groups. In a city that worshipped money, the poor were not just forgotten, but no longer had any place in the debate. It was time to fix this.

Missy's party had been the last surviving one still daring to campaign for a more equitable society, but some strands of their manifesto—such as the line asking for domestic helpers to be treated like other human beings—had resulted in them losing support. But their courage had made them friends across a wide range of people of different classes and cultures.

The young woman sprinted across the junction next to the HSBC headquarters and found the Queen of Statue Square sitting on a cardboard box with a flask of soup next to her, surrounded by acolytes. The indisputable matriarch and spiritual mother of the domestic-helper community was an old woman named Carmelita-Maria Macaraeg, said to be one of the most powerful people in the city. With two hundred thousand people in her network, many of whom were well-educated, and almost all of whom were working in the homes of—and privy to the secrets of—the most powerful people in Hong Kong, it was quite believable.

The Queen, who looked about seventy, sat with a scarf tied around her head, puffing at a cigar. She put it out, listened carefully to Missy's list of woes, and then picked up her flask of soup. She helped herself to several spoonsful before offering a response.

'You think you have two problems to deal with, but it's actually only one. We all have to clean house tonight, and you and your team have a particularly big job, I understand. And you have to find your friend's daughter, who seems to have been taken by a bad person, although you don't know that for sure. It seems like two unconnected things, but my feeling is that you need to focus on the main job, which is cleaning house, and the other problem will be solved as well. All problems are solved in the mind, you know. Ultimately.'

Missy listened politely, but not without frustration. Normally, she could deal with Carmelita-Maria's rambling platitudes, but tonight she was short of patience.

'But what do we do?' she asked. 'What can I do? I can't just put that problem aside. You know what Ric Fu Da Xin might do to her.'

'First, calm down. Without you being calm, there's no way you can use your biggest weapon: your head.'

Missy shook her head. 'My brain stopped working long ago. It's frozen in panic. I need to be doing something.'

After a pause, during which she examined the young Hong Kong woman's face, the old woman showed her gap-toothed smile. 'Okay, how about we get all practical, that's what you want, right? I'll make some calls, sort out the Menuka situation. You go clean house.'

Missy nodded. That was what she wanted to hear. 'Who will you put on it?'

'Don't know. I'm thinking Pyscho Bong.'

'Psycho?' The Chinese woman's eyes widened.

Carmelita-Maria raised one hand to forestall complaints. 'You don't know Psycho like I do. Mostly he's useless for anything, but this time, I think he might be what we need.'

The old woman looked Missy steadily in the eye. The younger woman knew exactly what that meant: *trust me.*

Missy gulped. Then she said: 'Okay. Thank you.'

She turned and walked smartly away.

\*

Grace reckoned she could get some important calls done early if she combined them with her next two jobs: prepare Grandma Cheuk's list of bedtime medicines, and deal with the sick dog, who was dropping small puddles of vomit and poo in corners of the apartment.

Clicking on her tiny phone, she went to the small medicine cabinet built into the fridge. She assembled a selection of pills and placed them on a tray with a cup of warm Horlicks, calling Missy So as she worked. 'What'd she say?'

'She told us to focus on our house-cleaning jobs,' Missy replied, a rhythmic tremor in her voice revealing that she was marching at high speed while talking. 'And she's going to sort out the Menuka problem herself.'

'What's she going to do? I'll need to tell Arunalatha. She's beside herself.'

There was a pause before Missy answered. 'She's putting Psycho on it.'

Grace took a sharp breath. 'That's an… odd choice.'

'Yes. Better not tell Arunalatha.'

'Yes.'

Boy 'Psycho' Bong de Rosales was a very capable man, but he had an unfortunate penchant for molesting young women, twice having been jailed for that offence. Since Menuka had been delivered into the hands of a well-known predator, Psycho was surely unsuited for the role of rescuer. Out of the frying pan?

Two minutes later Arunalatha, having been briefly informed that the finest staff of the Queen of Statue Square were confident of recovering her daughter, Grace turned her to attention to her employer's mother, who lived in the next apartment.

Half an hour later, Grandma Cheuk's wants having been tended to, Grace got down to her next job: locating the pools of dog vomit and diarrhoea. She followed her nose, before dropping to her knees with a cloth, bucket, and mop. As she went from glutinous pool to glutinous pool, she thought, *How could one small animal produce so much stuff?*

As she mentally prepared herself for the events of later tonight, her mind ran over the history of the multi-national group she now liked to think of as 'her people'. In the 1970s, Hong Kong servants were Chinese women called 'black and whites' because of their uniform: black pyjama-style trousers and white tunics. By the late 1980s, they had almost all been replaced by women from the Philippines after Hong Kong parents realised that Filipinas spoke fluent English and would save them a fortune on language tutors. By 2000, Indonesians and Sri Lankans had entered the market, under-cutting the Filipinas on price. By 2020, there were other nationalities, including staff from Bangladesh, and later, Cambodia and Vietnam. By the 2030s, most of the region's major urban centres, including Manila, had pummelled their economies into some sort of shape. So the middlemen seeking domestic staff had moved from the major cities to the poorer regions—sourcing workers from the outlying parts of Indonesia, the poorer states of the Philippines, the rural parts of Burma and Laos. Grace herself had been born in Davao Oriental.

In Hong Kong, there was a general belief that when 1 July 2047 arrived, domestic helpers would be quietly packed back to their original homes as their contracts ended, to be replaced by women from mainland China, as that country also had a large rural population needing gainful employment. One way or another, life would definitely change tonight.

Once the floors were scrubbed and the dog settled in his sleeping basket, Grace looked at the time on her phone screen. She put the bucket and mop away.

A few minutes later, the Cheuk family's domestic helper sat in her tiny room, and quietly turned on all her tools. In addition to her bluetooth phone, she had a laptop and two other mobiles, out-of-date models bought cheaply or given to her.

Using various conference-call facilities, she managed to get a circle of nearly forty individuals on standby. 'It's time to start cleaning the house,' she wrote in a message to all of them.

*

The full house-cleaning team actually numbered more than seven hundred members, but the core team which would be operating tonight consisted of forty-two individuals.

Each controlled a key function and had between three and four people helping. Grace had been on the two top teams, the legal one and the tech side—and at this moment, the second was her focus.

With half an hour to go before she needed to stand by for serious action, she put together a list of things that needed double-checking. One of her phones rang.

It was Yuliana, an Indonesian in her early twenties. 'I must drop out in ten minutes,' she said. 'My employer's family is coming. Boss told me, wash their cars, all of them.'

'We've got you backed up,' Grace said. 'Felicia will cover for you.'

'Thank you. What stage are we at now? It'll work okay, you

think?'

'We've already done the key moves. It's really all in play at the moment. It's up to the tech team now.'

'Can you explain it to me again? How it's going to work?'

Grace glanced at the clock. She had time to talk it through. She explained that a committee of top government lawyers had prepared a document to link the legal and economic systems of Hong Kong and China. It would come into force at exactly midnight tonight, 1 July 2047.

The key document, agreed in principle with their counterparts in Beijing, was simply called 'the Schedule' for short. But the lawyers on the Hong Kong side were anxious to be seen as heroes, so they prepared various alternative versions of it, which introduced perceived advantages for their community.

At first, Samuel Cheuk had been hopeful that they would get the Beijingers to agree to Schedule 07 or 08. But as the intransigence of the Beijing side became apparent, the Hong Kong side backed off. Eventually Samuel Cheuk promised the chief executive that he would get the Beijingers to sign Schedule 02—this was identical to the originally agreed draft except for a single unimportant word. Earlier that week, at a final meeting, Cheuk had pleaded with his counterpart over the matter. 'It's just one word different,' he had said. 'And it's not even a significant word. It just gives me face.' But even this humiliating plea had left the Beijing side unmoved. And so Samuel Cheuk had sent the bad news back to his team. 'Use the first schedule.'

Tonight, at midnight, the principals would sign the 'paper' (actually a Lenovo-sponsored touch screen) using gold styli (sponsored by Montblanc Asia Pacific). Soft copies would be instantly transmitted to more than seventy-three thousand parties who had registered an interest.

Yuliana said, 'Only there are many surprises in the document, yes?'

Grace breathed out slowly. 'God willing,' she sighed.

Dozens of highly skilled people, working in the homes of the most powerful individuals in Hong Kong, had done a major editing job, with the whole operation coordinated by the house cleaners' legal team. Since so many domestic helpers had higher degrees in law, international affairs, and other areas, it wasn't difficult to rewrite the document professionally, especially since sympathetic Hongkongers from one of last remaining democratic party had joined the operation. The new document had been masterminded by Chrisanto de Ramos (international affairs, computer science), Arunalatha Banda (international law), Missy So Hoi-shun (politics and Chinese law), and Adrianti Wiharjo (ethics and philosophy).

A Hong Kong democrat named Ling Wai-man and a Sri Lankan driver named Shehan Gamage had been in charge of hacking the government's computer systems. They had simply input the new file into the system as Schedule 00. It looked exactly the same for the first three pages, and also for the final page, where the principals would sign. But in the body of the document were a number of important changes—which would become apparent later.

'The team has spent almost three years planning the coup. And now we're down to the final hours,' Grace told Yuliana.

The final implementation team of forty-two house cleaners included people of twelve nations, including Hongkongers, Filipinos, Sri Lankans, Indonesians, Bangladeshis, Indians, Malaysians, Burmese, Mainland Chinese, Cambodians, Vietnamese, and a Laotian.

*

The phone rang at 10.53pm.

It was Alex Ng Chun-nam, a supporter who had been drawn into the covert operation by Missy So. 'Grace? Missy and I are just going into the handover ceremony but she asked me to tell you. Menuka's free.'

Grace closed her eyes. '*Salamat Hesus*,' she gasped. 'Is she okay?'

'She's fine.'

'What happened?'

'I don't know any details,' the young man said. 'But Missy got a call from the Queen.'

Grace rang off and immediately dialled Carmelita-Maria Macaraeg's number for confirmation. The Queen of Statue

Square rarely answered the phone, preferring her 'subjects' to visit her in person, but Grace hoped she would make an exception tonight, or one of her acolytes might answer the phone for her.

'*Bakit?*' a deep, raspy voice said.

'Ms Macaraeg? It's Grace Inday Masipag. Is Menuka okay?'

The old woman cackled. '*Okay lang huwag kang mag alala.*'

'She's not been... harmed in any way?'

'Pure as the day she was born. Well, no, better revise that, as pure as she was this morning.'

'*Salamat.*' Grace wanted to start dialling Arunalatha's number on the other phone, but the old matriarch felt the need to add details: 'Apparently Ric was hungry for a treat on this special occasion so his men took Menuka to their boss's main Hong Kong dungeon. He's calling it the Party Room.'

'Go on.'

'So the girl is presented to the rapist-in-charge. The beast looks her up-down, sees her fishnet stockings, her retropunk stud things, all that. And then he waves his hand. "Take her away," he says. "She look like she wants it. I don't want no girls who want it. I only want girls who don't want it." Then the men just dump her outside. One of my people just saw her and call me.'

'*Salamat sa panginoon.*'

'Thank God? I think she can thank her nose ring.'

\*

The minutes ticked by achingly slowly.

On telemedia screens, various symbolic exchanges took place among political leaders, and pundits over-analysed each action, statement, and nose-scratch.

As midnight hove into view, Grace ran through her team's task once more with Alex Ng.

'You just stand by from now on,' Alex said. 'At 11.52, Missy So and myself will get into the e-documents room of the convention centre's tech team. There we meet Lai Kin-ming, a sympathiser. He will disable Schedule 01. He knows how to do that without setting off any alarms. He will upload Schedule 00 in its place. If for any reason this fails to occur, we move to Plan B and send a message to Ling and Gamage.'

'Okay. Got that.'

'Then it's all down to you. Since there are signal jammers surrounding the building, we can't call you, and you can't call us. So from 11.58 onwards, you have to watch the TV ceremony carefully. Gamage will turn off the firewalls through a pre-arranged access point. As he does this, Ling will use a small, smuggled-in flash camera to take a picture of the proceedings. It will flash three times in quick succession. Cameras are banned from the room, so hopefully there will be no false signals to confuse you. You will be watching television at home, and you will see a triple camera flash. At that moment, you will upload Schedule 00, using the high-security private access cable that your employer has. It's the only other cable with access to the government's top security legal server.'

'I understand.' The words *it's all down to you* reverberated worryingly in her skull.

'The firewall will only down for three or four seconds, because after five seconds, an alarm will sound. So you *must* upload it the moment you see the three high-speed camera flashes, okay? Flash-flash-flash. Press enter. Don't delay.'

Grace breathed in and out slowly. 'I understand,' she repeated.

He rang off.

The phone immediately rang again. 'Carmelita here. Just thought you'd like to know. Menuka's now home with her mother. Happy ending.'

The domestic helper closed her eyes. 'Thank you, *God*,' she said.

'You're welcome,' the one woman cackled.

One challenge solved, one more to go. Grace turned her attention back to the ceremonies on the screen.

Then she heard a sound behind her.

\*

Ric Fu Da Xin stood in the doorway to the domestic helper's room, a dark, cruel smile on his face. He had a doctor's bag in one hand. He lowered it to the ground. It was heavy. What was inside? Tools of some sort?

'Hello, Grace,' he said, his voice flat and monotone. 'How nice to see you.'

'Oh, uh, nice to see you, too. But my—my employer's not, not here,' the domestic helper stuttered. 'He's at the ceremony. You want to see Mr Cheuk?'

'Actually, no,' Ric said. 'I'm here to see you.'

Grace had seen him at close quarters twice at dinner parties arranged by her employer. Fu had always been smartly dressed and smiling. But she could see from the way his expensive suit hugged his shoulders that he had a hard, muscular body, and his grin was an evil grimace.

'Can I get you anything? A drink?' she said, standing up. Fear stiffened her movements.

He slowly shook his head. 'You're not going anywhere.'

'Would-would-would you like a cup of tea, Mr Fu?' she stammered, suddenly hot.

He held up his hand to signify that she shouldn't move. 'I've had my eye on you for a long time,' he said. 'Religious, right? Always wear a cross? I think you'd rather be a nun than a helper, right? That's what Samuel told me.'

She lowered her head and smiled. 'Yes, that's right. I plan to go into an order after finishing this job.'

He took a step closer to her.

She glanced down at his right hand and noticed his knuckles turn white as he clenched his fist.

Grace Inday Masipag shuddered and tensed.

*

At exactly 11.52, Missy So and Alex Ng stepped breathlessly into the control room. 'Here's the file,' Missy said in Cantonese, showing a tiny drive. 'To upload.'

Lai Kin-ming didn't move, didn't take it.

'You have to upload it. Now. Please. We have little time.'

Lai lifted both palms too her, fear in his eyes. 'I don't know. I don't know.'

Alex stepped forwards. 'We've got no time for this. You can't change your mind now. Upload the file.'

Lai shook his head. 'I don't know. We are going to get into so much trouble!'

Alex clenched his teeth and grabbed Lai by the lapels. 'We don't have time to talk,' he said.

'You do it then,' said Lai.

Alex peered at the walls of solid state technology. There was no way he could work out what to do.

Missy said: 'Let him go, Alex. Let me talk to him.'

She motioned for Lai to sit down, and pulled up a chair so she could sit facing him. 'I know we're asking a lot from you, but it's really important you help us now.'

Lai asked, 'What exactly is on Schedule 00? Are you giving away our country to foreigners? I'm scared that's what you're doing—and I'll get the blame.'

'We've told you so many times,' Alex shouted.

Missy spoke quietly. 'No. We're doing exactly the opposite. We've explained this to you before, but I'm happy to explain it again. There are some changes to the law in our revised version of the schedule—changes that will benefit all of us.'

He stared at her.

Missy continued, speaking with exaggerated calm. 'This document turns Hong Kong into World City Number One. A free state. The world's first totally free state. All the free access and open channels that function in the business arena in this city will be transferred to the human arena. Goods have always flowed in and out of Hong Kong freely, but in a controlled manner. From now on, human beings will do the same. Hong Kong will become an open society, a true meritocracy.'

'Instead of joining with China, you'll be making Hong Kong independent?'

'No. Not at all. Our borders with China will relax, just as planned. But so will our borders with the rest of the world—in *exactly* the same way.'

She took his hands in hers as she continued. 'We've taken the best practices in open-border agreements from around the world and implemented them in Hong Kong. It will become a borderless city. There'll be the necessary controls, to stop the place being flooded with warm bodies. But Hong Kong will be a new type of city. The world will be our country.'

'What if all this turns out to be bullshit?'

'It won't. Think of the role this place has played ever since it started to exist. It's the meeting place of East and West. It's where capitalism and communism meet. This is one of the youngest big-city communities in the world, in the heart of one of the oldest societies in the world. It's a clear-sighted, business-minded place, but it's also a place where society still leaves room for magical intangible things, like feng shui and numerology. It's a place with a huge amount of money, yet it has an extremely low crime rate. This is where all the planet's extremes all meet. Hong Kong is perfectly suited to be a model city for a new, borderless planet Earth.'

Lai said nothing. Beside her, Missy could feel Alex's panic as the time ticked by.

Then the technician spoke. 'But what will actually happen?'

'There's a list of seventy-three articles that define the changes in detail.'

'Like what?'

'Well, there are laws here which will fix certain anomalies. Let me give you an example. A model city must be for the people who live in it, it can't be a plaything for property speculators thousands of kilometres away. So speculators will be gradually cut out of the market. No more towers full of empty apartments no one can afford to rent.'

'But won't that cause a crash in the property market? That's what the government always says. It will cause a market crash.'

'No. It'll cause a distortion to disappear. That's not the same thing. Property in a city needs to be for people to live in, not for billionaires who live on the other side of the planet to flip for profit.'

There was a silence, while Lai looked at his hands. Then he looked up sharply at Missy. 'What else?'

Missy smiled. 'Billionaires pay less tax than middle class people. If this is going to be a world city of the future, we need to change all that: no more tax loopholes. Hong Kong tycoons who put all their assets in the Cayman Islands will have to stop pretending

151

they are patriotic Hongkongers and go live in the Cayman Islands. Nor will tycoons be allowed to hide secret stashes of money in Switzerland or places like that.'

'What else?' Lai asked.

Alex interrupted. 'We don't have time for this. You can't go through all seventy-three articles.'

Missy looked at him. 'We don't have time *not* to do this.' She turned back to Lai. 'But Alex is right, I can't go through the whole thing. You have to trust me. The new rules fix a lot of anomalies that have caused Hong Kong to drift away from its essential character.'

'I don't know what that means.'

'Hong Kong was born to be an international meeting place, a model city. Not just another Chinese town. Schedule 00 will codify Hong Kong's personality, its uniqueness, its quintessential nature. I'll give you one more example, then you need to help us. After Schedule 00 is signed, anyone who lives here seven years can become a permanent resident.'

'I thought we already had that.'

'No. We have that law for some people, but not for others. If you're an investment banker who flies around the world with all your assets in the Cayman Islands, you can get citizenship. But if you're a domestic helper who has spent every day of your working life here, you're denied this right. Hong Kong law has long had an exemption clause which is at odds with international law.'

'That change will be good for the helpers, but bad for Hong Kong.'

Missy shook her head. 'No. Many helpers have amazing qualifications—and often in areas where Hong Kong has a shortage. Let me give you an example. This city has had a severe shortage of nurses for years. We desperately need people in the caring professions. Yet the people who are perfectly trained, ready and willing to fix this need cannot do so, because of a law that is in itself illegal.'

'You're really doing this for Hong Kong people?'

'Yes. We don't want to be just another small town in China. So, as well as opening Hong Kong inward to China, we open it outward to the rest of the world.'

'Foreigners will be in charge?'

'No. Hong Kong people. At the moment, we have fake democracy, like most of Asia. Special interest groups dominate Legco, Exco, and all the so-called selection committees and advisory committees and electoral colleges. This new system will cancel all that at a stroke. And replace it with the simplest system of all. One person, one vote. Finally.'

Alex put his watch in front of Lai's face. 'It's now or never.'

Behind him, the door clicked open.

Two uniformed officers entered the room. 'Unauthorised people are not allowed in this area. You must come with us.' Both were armed.

Alex clapped his palm over his forehead in an expression of despair. As he did so, he whispered into his phone watch to send a message to a colleague elsewhere in the building. 'Ng to Ling: Go to Plan B. Repeat: Go to Plan B.'

A network of contacts quickly took the message outside of the signal jamming range where it was transmitted to an apartment in Mid-Levels.

*

Ric Fu Da Xin took a step closer to Grace.

Her eye was caught by a sudden change in the light from the computer screen. *Implement Plan B* started flashing on the screen.

The domestic helper stopped breathing. 'Please,' she said. 'Please.'

His eyebrows lifted. 'What?' he said. 'You don't want it?' His smile deepened, started to become genuine.

As she realised what was about to happen, pain flooded her system. Not horror for her own fate, but for the failure of the mission, for all their dreams and ambitions crumbling to nothing, for everything they'd worked for leading nowhere.

Her mobile phone started to ring. Ric Fu Da Xin picked it up and tossed it behind him, where it smashed on the tiled kitchen floor. There was silence in the house.

'God save us,' Grace whispered. '*Hesus.*'

The intruder leaned down to his bag and fumbled in it for

something.

And that's when she heard a voice. She would rather that it had been the voice of Jesus, but if it was Him, He was using the vocal chords of raspy-voiced old woman who had smoked cigars for most of her life. 'Tell him you want it,' said the voice.

Grace had forgotten that she was still wearing the hidden earpiece, and she was still plugged into the line of Carmelita-Maria Macaraeg, Queen of Statue Square. The old woman repeated: 'Tell him you want it.'

Grace forced her cheeks to rise. 'Hello, Mr Fu,' she said, trying to make her voice light and musical. 'When I say it's nice to see you, I really mean it. Last time you came to dinner here, I noticed you. I couldn't take my eyes off you.' She tried to still the tremor in her voice.

He stared at her, unmoving.

The Queen whispered in her ear: '*I want you to fuck me.*'

The domestic helper continued, trying not to babble: 'I've been thinking of you. You so handsome. Big muscles. I want you to fuck me.' She'd never said the phrase before, and it felt strange and powerful and bitter in her mouth, like when you accidently taste perfume. 'I really do.'

His brow knotted.

She beckoned him with her hand. What did people say in movies when they tried to seduce men? *Come here, big boy?* Would that sound right, coming from her mouth?

Then Ric Fu Da Xin's forehead smoothed itself and he smiled. 'You're trying to trick me, right? You're trying to make me believe you want it? You bitch. I'm going to make you pay for that.'

Grace forced the fear down, made herself keep smiling. 'The only people who are being fooled are the people who see the outside Grace and not the real me. The one who wants you.'

The Queen whispered in her ear. '*Show him your tits. Tell him you want his big fat cock inside you.*'

She pulled her shirt open, buttons flying off. 'I want your big fat cock.'

He stopped and stared at her breasts, a cloud passing over his face. For a moment he stood still, pondering, puzzling. Then he gave a real smile. 'Clever,' he said. 'Real clever.'

He stepped forwards. As he reached her, she moved backwards, stumbling over a small stool and falling to the ground. She took a moment to gather her senses. When she and looked up, she saw he had a thick rope in his hands. She closed her eyes and braced herself.

*

There was a loud crash—and then another one. Opening her eyes, she saw two men struggling on the floor. Ric Fu Da Xin was on the floor. On top of him, a small, stocky, spiky-haired man was energetically battering his face.

'*Salamat*,' Grace said in a tiny voice.

'Don't thank me,' Psycho Bong said. 'You got work to do. Go clean house.'

She raced to the computer.

As she reached the screen, she saw it was 11.58:31. Less than ninety seconds left. She needed to watch for the signal to upload Schedule 00 to the system.

She immediately realised that she and her team-mates had screwed up a key part of the plan. No cameras were allowed but clearly lots of people were ignoring the rule—as the principals walked to the centre of the stage, a stream of camera flashes lit up the scene. She had no way of knowing which were the ones that signalled the short break when the firewall was down, the brief window during which she had to upload the file that would turn Hong Kong into World City Number One.

She scanned the screen feverishly, looking for something that might be a triple flash as described to her. She saw a slightly staggered burst of light and thought that might be it. But had it been three flashes? Or just two?

Her right hand instinctively reached for the cross that dangled in front of her chest.

'Nice tits,' she heard Psycho say from the floor.

'Help me, Jesus, Mary, and Joseph,' she prayed, using her left hand to pull her shirt over her breasts. 'It's up to you. *Tulongan mo ako, panginoon.*'

She closed her eyes and pressed Enter.

## Notes on the Contributors

**Yeung Chak Yan** was born and grew up in Hong Kong. She holds a B.Sc. in Computer Science from the Chinese University of Hong Kong and an M.A. in Creative Writing from Bath Spa University. She currently lives in Hong Kong, exploring the field of computational linguistics while writing a novel.

**Jenn Chan Lyman** is a fiction and non-fiction writer based in Shanghai, with roots in Hong Kong and California. Jenn has a B.A. in Comparative Literature from Stanford University (1999) and an M.F.A. in Creative Writing from City University of Hong Kong (2012). Selected publishing credits and accolades include Finalist for *Glimmer Train*'s May 2012 Short Story Award for New Writers, publication in *Salamander Magazine*, and a Pushcart Prize nomination in 2013.

**Stephanie Han** (M.A., M.F.A.) is City University of Hong Kong's first Ph.D. student in English literature. Her creative work has appeared in *DisOrient*, *The Kyoto Journal*, *Louisville Review*, *The South China Morning Post* (Fiction Award), *Nimrod International Literary Journal* (Fiction Award), *Santa Fe Writer's Project* (Fiction Award), *Women's Studies Quarterly*, *Cha Online Journal*, *Ampersand Review* and other publications. Her writing has been anthologised in PEN West's anthology, *Strange Cargo*, and the Asian American Women Artists Anthology, *Cheers to Muses*, and will be anthologised in *The Tao of Parenthood* and *How Does One Dress to Buy Dragonfruit?*. Her literary criticism has appeared in *Contemporary Women's Writing* and *The Explicator*. She lives in Mui Wo, Lantau, Hong Kong: see **www.stephaniehan.com**.

**Peter J. Phillips** Peter is a Sydney-born writer and teacher who has lived in Hong Kong for the past seven years. In 2012, he received his M.F.A. in fiction from City University of Hong Kong, where he has also lectured in the English Department. He currently teaches English at a secondary school and is passionate about promoting creative writing to Hong Kong's youth. He has been a finalist in the *Indiana Review*'s 1/2K Prize and his fiction has been published in *Cha: An Asian Literary Journal*. Phillips is a proud resident of Happy Valley and has lived within earshot of its racetrack since his arrival in Hong Kong.

**Ploy Pirapokin** was born in Bangkok, Thailand, and relocated to Hong Kong when she was six. She is presently an M.F.A. Fiction candidate at San Francisco State University and has attended a writing residency at the City University of Hong Kong. She graduated in 2010 with a Bachelor of Arts degree in Communication Studies and English from the University of San Diego. She has worked as a journalist and a copywriter, and has contributed articles for *Discover San Diego*, *Allied Advertising*, *Ask Miss A,* and the *Daily Deal Media*. She has been a part of the Editorial staff of *Fourteen Hills: A San Francisco State Review*, and her fiction has been featured as part of the Asian American Women's Artists Association's 16th Annual United States of Asian America Festival. She currently lives in San Francisco and is working on short fiction and novels grounded in Hong Kong, focusing on themes such as identity development, third-culture kids, and coming-of-age stories.

**Ysabelle Cheung** is a writer, editor, and illustrator from London, now in Hong Kong. Since graduating from the University of East Anglia with a Creative Writing degree, she has contributed to various publications including *Granta, Tatler Asia*, and *Asia Literary Review*. Her current positions include Art, Culture and Clubbing Editor of *Time Out Hong Kong*; manager of monthly literary night Liars' League Hong Kong; and contributor to the graphite artzine, *Tiny Pencil*. She is currently working on an illustrated novella.

**Jason Y. Ng** was born in Hong Kong, but spent his adult life in Europe and North America before settling in his birthplace to rediscover his roots. He is a full-time lawyer, a magazine columnist, and a resident blogger for the *South China Morning Post*. His social commentary blog, *As I See It,* and leisure review site *The Real Deal*, have attracted a cult following. Ng is the bestselling author of *Hong Kong State of Mind* (2010) and *No City for Slow Men* (2013). He has been featured at the Hong Kong Book Fair and the Hong Kong International Literary Festival. For more information, visit **www.jasonyng.com**.

**Nury Vittachi** is the author of more than three dozen books. Born in Sri Lanka, he settled in Hong Kong in the 1980s, adopting three local Chinese children. His bibliography includes books published in Chinese, Hindi, English, Spanish, and Indonesian. Vittachi is founder-editor of the region's top literary journal, the *Asia Literary Review*, and chairman of Asia Pacific Writers, the region's largest author association. His works have been issued by major publishers in Asia, the US, the UK, Europe and Australia.

## Notes on the Editors

**Marshall Moore i**s the author of seven books, including the novels *Bitter Orange* (2013) and *The Concrete Sky* (2003), and the collection *The Infernal Republic* (2012). A native of eastern North Carolina, he has been a resident of Hong Kong for six years. He teaches at Lingnan University. For more information, please **visit www.marshallmoore.com** or follow him on Twitter at **@articulateink**.

**Xu Xi (許素細)** is the author of nine books of fiction and essays. Recent titles are *Access: Thirteen Tales* (2011), the novel *Habit of a Foreign Sky* (2010) (which was shortlisted for the inaugural Man Asian Literary Prize), and the essay collection *Evanescent Isles: from my city-village* (2008). She is also editor of three anthologies of Hong Kong writing in English and is the regional Hong Kong editor of the Routledge's *Encyclopedia of Post-Colonial Literature,* 2nd ed. Awards include an O. Henry prize story, a New York Foundation of the Arts fiction fellowship, and first place in the *South China Morning Post* short story contest, as well as several distinguished writer-in-residence positions at universities and artists' colonies worldwide. From 2002 to 2012, she was on the faculty at the Masters of Fine Arts (M.F.A.) in writing at Vermont College of Fine Arts, where she was elected and served as faculty chair from 2009 to 2012. In 2010, she was named writer-in-residence at City University of Hong Kong, Department of English, where she founded and directs Asia's first low-residency MFA in creative writing. Please visit her at **www.xuxiwriter. com, www.facebook.com/XuXiWriter**, and **@xuxiwriter**.

Made in the USA
Middletown, DE
05 December 2022